The Rise of Caesar

by

August Sommers

Seventeen years had come and gone at Three Winds Plantation. And overall the years had been prosperous for most of the colored ex-slaves. Oh, there had been some resistance the first few years. Despite the word that the niggras at Three Winds were well trained and heavily armed there were still those bands of night riders who believed in their air of supremacy and wrestled with the fact that no niggas slaves could outwit or had the nerve to put up any formidable resistance against Confederate soldiers who'd had the honor of fighting under General Jefferson Davis. These were outsiders mostly.

The good folks of Jackson had already come up against the niggras of Three Winds and had, in the end, decided it best to leave them niggras alone once the evening raids turned into skirmishes and then battles with them counting heavy losses. They had just lost one war and if the gods weren't with them then there was little chance they'd win this one either.

Three years later, they'd seen more than enough killing and bloodshed to come to the realization that white or not these niggras was not going to just hand over the land and were fighting for not only their sons and daughters but for their own survival.

Yes, it had taken three long years for those good southern white folks of Jackson to come to the realization that the best they could ask for was to sort of co-exist with the niggras from Three Winds. And so they had come to be at peace with each other and to come to grips with the fact that the niggras at Three Winds were no more than an anomaly and of course as we all know anomalies are allowed to exist but are no more than that; something out of the norm.

Still, word of niggra slaves running one of the largest plantations in Mississippi traveled quickly. White Mississippians still so entrenched in their own hatred and bigotry still had a hard time with the idea that these ex-slaves were surpassing many a white man following the war.

It was these that now came to see if these here niggras were for real. They were quickly thwarted by superior numbers and one of the best military strategists Black or white and would soon turn tail and run still maintaining that air of superiority only to return soon thereafter in greater numbers only to meet with the same peril.

Jeremiah who had taken over as council president and military general had spent the great majority of his adulthood under Andrew's tutelage was now commandeering the military forces. Always curious as to learning the finer points in the art of war Jeremiah under the careful guidance of Andrew studied all the great military leaders. He studied Alexander the Great, Genghis Khan and Hannibal infusing all of their methods and strategies in training the troops of Three Winds. Introducing guerilla warfare to their arsenal on a land they were all too familiar with it was possible he may have assembled the greatest peacetime army aside from the U.S. government that had ever been assembled on American soil. With close to four thousand men troops at the ready there was hardly an army that stood a chance. And still they came.

The raids and attacks on Three Winds had all but dissipated in recent years but there was always the threat and so they stayed ready, mobilized. And it was Andrew who by now had relinquished almost all of his duties with the council and only acted as a personal consultant to Jeremiah when called upon who first approached the matter one evening.

"Jeremiah, my brother, how long have we known each other?"

Knowing Andrew all his life he knew that whatever was coming was of a serious nature and obviously something Andrew wanted so badly he was going to bring up their friendship and brotherhood.

"You and I both know the answer to that Andrew. So what is it that is on your mind my brother?"

Andrew had to smile as he pulled deeply on the corncob pipe. He wondered how many years he and Jeremiah had spent on this front porch in the dawn of the evening to mull over the day and the politics that had now become a part of Three Winds society.

They had grown to a community of some sixty thousand and with the growth came demands and problems they had not known in simpler times. And there were other nights that demanded little and they shared talk of their children. Jeremiah and Fiona now in their mid-fifties had eight children while Andrew and Petunia were not far behind with seven.

Andrew exhaled letting the wind grab hold of the smoke whisking it away into the warm summer's air. Andrew smiled. Jeremiah had always been a man of deep thought and few words. Why he thought he could pull the wool over his old friend's eyes seemed ludicrous now. But Andrew still held the welfare of Three Winds in his hands and though he'd delegated much of the responsibility to those most capable around him he was still responsible for the overall direction of Three Winds.

"Jeremiah how many men do you have under your command at present."

"A little over four thousand and I'd say another two hundred in our Special Unit."

"That's the guerilla unit you composed? In all honesty Andrew, I think this unit alone could defeat any attack against Three Winds."

"And when we started out twenty years ago that was basically all we had. And two hundred men were sufficient."

"It was."

"Now we have four thousand. That's what bothers me. I was thinking that we could cut that number in half. The sheer numbers are starting to become a financial burden. The money alone in stipends for males serving two years has become a cumbersome weight to carry and some of those funds can be put towards other projects which are in need of development. The library, school, and hospital are all in need of repair and improvement."

"No argument here. But to release two thousand men into the community with no other viable skills could really send shockwaves throughout Three Winds. What would they do?"

"Thought about that and I think we can continue to pay them. What are they getting now…ten dollars a month? Well, let's continue to pay them but what I'd like to see happen is a trade school go up and instead of their entire day being spent preparing for an enemy we may never see let's put these men to work doing something constructive that will in turn help Three Winds to reach its full potential. We need schools. Four maybe five at each corner of Three Winds. We can hardly contain the children we have in those makeshift lean twos. Our church is an open field and our hospital and library are undersized. I think the people will understand and still feel adequately protected with an army of two thousand men."

"We have a council meeting tonight. I'll run it by them then. I understand your concerns my brother and I feel the need but you know a few of the young men who didn't have a particular affinity for school may not be too happy about this. A lot of them look at this as their sole profession and take pride in soldiering. They'll be the hardest to convince."

"Change is difficult for all of us but without change there is no progress."

"I agree but I thought you should know this will not go over without some grumbling."

"At my age I've come to expect grumbling. How are Fiona and the kids doing?"

"Couldn't be better. My baby girl Cynthia just turned seventeen and finished up her schooling here and was accepted into college in Boston. Said she wants to go and study medicine."

"That's a beautiful thing my friend."

"Yes, it is but Boston is so very far away and here's a child that has never been beyond Natchez."

Andrew smiled.

"Why are you smiling Andrew?"

"Just reminiscing a little is all. It wasn't so long ago that we were also thinking of leaving this place. I remember you and me talking to poppa about sneaking away from here and going to New Orleans to hire on a ship as cabin boys so we could throw the shackles of slavery off and see the world. Do you remember the look on poppas face?"

Jeremiah smiled.

"You had that same look on your face just a minute ago when you were telling me about Cynthia. That's why I was smiling."

"I hear you. I guess we've become our parents. Speaking of which your son Caesar reminds me so much of you as a young man, Andrew. It's downright scary."

Andrew dropped his head. He'd never come to grips with the fact that he'd fathered a son by his own sister and at Fiona's request had not had a hand in raising him. The boy had grown up under Jeremiah's tutelage and though Andrew checked on him periodically he'd done no more than he'd done for the rest of the children of Three Winds.

"You know he was also a good student and voracious reader but when he was finished with school he readily accepted his two years of mandatory military service without so much as a peep.

What's more is he was our finest recruit and was one of the reasons Fiona and I set up the guerilla branch of the army. He just had so much more to offer than the typical recruit and he went above and beyond. He's one hell of a marksman so I put him with the snipers. He excelled. I enrolled him in the martial arts. He excelled. I put him with our finest in hand-to-hand combat. He excelled. Now I have him leading his own regiment. And at twenty four he is now responsible for training others. To tell you the truth I don't know what else to do with him."

Andrew never raised his head afraid that his pride would show though he beamed with pride. Jeremiah knew his friend's turmoil and did his best to keep Andrew abreast of Caesar's growth over the years.

"He's really something that boy of yours but I'll tell you this Andrew. He's like a lot of boys his age that are vested. If we take the lure of his military duty away from him Lord knows what he'll end up doing or where he'll channel his energy."

Andrew smiled now seeing more clearly the reason for the latest update on Caesar.

"Not a problem my friend. His energies will now not only be concentrated on his military expertise but also on continuing his schooling. That should keep him focused and when there is a day where there is no need for guerillas on Three Winds he will have a trade and the know how to support himself and his family. It's almost the same as sending Cynthia away to attend medical school in Boston. We must prepare them to better themselves and their families."

"As I said I will let them know tonight at the council meeting," Jeremiah said standing and sipping the hooch before hugging Andrew tightly and bidding him farewell.

Andrew knew that Jeremiah was also feeling a certain type of way about decreasing the military but it was time for everyone to tighten up and pull in the reins.

Sure it would lessen Jeremiah's powers but that was the sacrifice he would have to make for the community as a whole. And Lord knows it seemed like his whole life had been a sacrifice of one sort or another for the sake of Three Winds. Jeremiah would just have to understand.

An hour later, Andrew stood up and drained what was left of the homemade hooch, knocked the ashes from his pipe and headed in.

"That you honey?"

"And who else would it be at this time of the night P?"

"Just checking," Petunia said taken back by her husband's attitude. "And what bug crawled up your ass tonight."

"Sorry P. I didn't mean to come off that way."

"From the tone of things I'm thinking you talked to Jeremiah about downsizing the military?"

"I did."

"And I guess he didn't take it well."

"I guess he took it as well as can be expected. For appearances sake I think he tried not to let it show but after ten years as council president and military commander I think he has come to the position that he is beyond reproach."

"I do believe that it goes back to the Machiavellian concept. Power corrupts and absolute power corrupts absolutely. He simply has too much power for one man. I think Jeremiah believes that it is he who controls Three Winds and though you brought him to this position you are now expendable. He owes you nothing."

"For his sake and mine I hope you're wrong my love."

"You and me both. Did you tell him about the plans for a new school, library and hospital as well as the fusion of many of the military into skilled laborers and artisans?"

"I did."

"And what was his response?"

"You don't want to know."

"Tell me Andrew."

"He played the only card open to him. He told me how Caesar had grown into one of his best soldiers and exceeded all expectations. He then went on to say that if I were to disband the military then Caesar and a lot of young men just like him would be without any sense of moral value or worth."

"Oh! That's low. Tell me he didn't try to use your own son against you?"

"I'm afraid he did."

"And what was your response?

"I simply explained to him that the council's has always believed that the needs of the many always supersede the needs of the individual. And now that we are coming to a point that we are tolerated as a community of ex-slaves meaning no harm to the surrounding communities a full time army will soon be unnecessary and that these young men would need a trade as they got older to provide for themselves and their families."

"And his reply?"

"He said he would bring it up to the council and let me know how they felt about it in the morning but I could tell that he wasn't in concert with the whole idea."

"Don't worry Andrew. I'll speak to Fiona in the morning. He may be a general at the council and among his troops but we know who the real commander in chief is when the lights get dim," Petunia said laughing heartily. "Just like you know who the real master of Three Winds is," she said summoning Andrew to her and kissing him passionately. "I love you Andrew."

Of that there had never been any question but she knew if her man had one flaw it was that he was bound by loyalty and threw caution to the wind if it meant questioning the allegiance of a friend.

No, to Andrew all the skirmishes and battles they had endured on the way to becoming masters of their own destinies was something Andrew would never question just as his father had never questioned the loyalty and allegiance of his council members. But in recent years the niggras at Three Winds had grown fat and comfortable and forgotten the struggle they had to endure to get where they were now. And after several years of good and better than average harvests there were those who seemingly forgot that it was Andrew who was solely responsible for their success and decided they were tired of this new master and set out to oppose him.

But it was Petunia and Fiona who acting independently of the council rounded up three or four of the ringleaders of this uprising and took them to a small clearing in the woods and hung the ringleader and promised the same to the others if they did not succumb to the law of the land. All had been peaceful following the hanging up until now but Petunia now felt the imminent threat even if Andrew still believed in the idea of friendship. In the case of Jeremiah he would never sanction any action but Andrew with his cornucopia of knowledge knew the history of man and mankind it was Petunia who knew men and the evil that lurked dormant masking itself in the cloak of friendship. And after half a century on this earth she'd worked too hard and too long to see anything happen to her man.

Andrew who at fifty-seven had long since retired from the classroom and the battlefield was for all intents and purposes content to watch his children grow and flourish into strong men and women. He was content working from behind the scenes implementing upgrades and maintenance to Three Winds. But the opposition he received when he tried to purchase and begin cultivation of another ten thousand acres of land to accommodate the many hundreds of now free niggras swarming to Three Winds seeking sanctuary was almost more than he could stand.

It was at this time, oh say five years ago, that Petunia and Fiona had quelled the disturbance without Andrew's knowledge. The uprising hurt him so after all he'd done and sacrificed that he turned a blind eye to the politics of Three Winds and became content with the job of raising his children. Well, that was until Petunia or Jeremiah came to him seeking his advice or prodded him to take the initiative on some project or other. This time it was Petunia who came forward suggesting what he already knew.

"Andrew sweetheart, I don't know if you've noticed or not but we have close to six thousand school aged children who we promised a quality education when we took over Three Winds ten years ago. We have three school houses that house forty children apiece. The rest are out in the fields on benches pretending to be getting an education. Most of them can barely read or write. If it rains there is no school. If it's too cold or snows there is no school. All of our talk of educating our children has become just that just talk. And you haven't lifted a hand towards addressing or rectifying the problem. It's as if you don't care or are just blind to what's going on on your own land. You worked hard to achieve all that we have. You and no one else is responsible for this. We supported you but it was you who laid the foundation. It was you who put the work in and it was you Missy Anne willed her land to. This is your land. I can remember a time when you were not yet even the council head and you and Jeremiah would go out and right a wrong, correct an injustice just because it was the right thing to do. Now because of a few ignorant, ungrateful, niggas who don't know the struggle you went through try to defy and undermine you on the way you run your land and you put your tail between your legs and run like a bitch in heat. Well, that's the not the Andrew I grew up with and fought to marry. The man I knew looked at struggle as nothing more than motivation.

Andrew heard his wife but could say nothing. He knew deep in his heart and soul that P. was right. He'd just not considered that after a lifetime of servitude for those that he had nothing in common with aside from the fact that they too were slaves that they would turn on him. It hurt to the quick that these very same brothers in bondage would rise to try and thwart and undermine all that he had done for him. It hurt deeply. But Petunia was right. This was his land and he would not only seek to cultivate the land but also the minds of those that occupied the land.

Yes, Petunia was right. He'd chosen to take a back seat when they came after him. Those same niggras would have readily accepted any suggestion or better yet order the Colonel would have given them with a drop of the head and a 'yassuh' but here they were living better than they ever had thanks primarily to him and as the saying goes these niggras were intent on 'biting the hand that fed them'.

Only a few years removed from being whipped, castrated and hung they'd forgotten. And then just as quickly they'd quelled their demands and merely dissipated into the ranks as far as he knew but they hadn't received any flack from him. It was at that point that he'd began to wonder how much fight he had left in him and conceded that he was not going to fight for his people and then have to fight them too. That was up until today when Petunia who knew her man better than anyone and knew how to elicit a reaction made him sit up.

It was Petunia who also knew and had the foresight to see that for every action there is an equal and opposite reaction. And so before triggering Andrew to act she sent out some feelers to get a feel for the response Andrew's proposals would get and though most were in agreement that there was room for much improvement she gathered that there would be some strong sentiment within the rank and file of the military.

Yet and still she knew that the military was under Jeremiah and a strong leader could make an unsavory decision seem almost palatable. Call it women's intuition but Petunia knew that as good a friend as Jeremiah was when it came down to self-preservation he would always look out for Jeremiah first and now that he held the keys to the throne he was hardly about to relinquish it for the good of the people.

At the same time, some six or seven miles away at the northernmost part of Three Winds there was a council meeting underway.

Ol' Ben who was now close to ninety years of age and now acted as only a consultant to Jeremiah listened impassionedly as Jeremiah addressed the crowd of close to a thousand men.

"The last order of business tonight is a matter which has grieved me deeply but it is my duty to relay it to you. It has been brought to my attention that Three Winds is in dire need of some much needed renovations. Schools as well as an addition to our hospital and libraries are sorely needed and it seems that the only way in which we are going to be able to procure these much needed additions is to make cuts in the army personnel."

A hush fell over the crowd most of whom were military before shouts and cries went up.

"No, no, no. Ahh… hell no."

"What are you saying Jeremiah? You can't cut the army."

"And what do you propose we do then?"

"Gentlemen! Gentlemen! If you would only let me finish. It has been proposed that you split your training days in half and a trade school will be set up for all of you to learn a trade and when there is no threat and the army is totally disbanded that you will have a trade and be able to secure employment so you can provide for your families. Think about it and let me know your thoughts. My door is always open. And if there is nothing else on the agenda I hope you all have a pleasant evening."

More jeers and grumbling could be heard through the crowd as the men discussed heatedly the talk of the dissolution of the army.

Ol' Ben in no hurry sat and listened to the idle chatter. A wise man who had spent close to a century in the council and was attuned to the political savvy and power plays of men much more renown than Jeremiah could immediately see what was transforming.

Yes Jeremiah had conveyed Andrew's message as he was told but he had by no means done anything to dissuade or lobby the men should they became heated over this latest bit of news.

Ben knew that a good leader who was on board would have gone to the ends of the earth to lobby his men to follow him. But Jeremiah had only laid it out there seemingly to incite his followers to reject this latest proposal. It was clearly the first time in the twenty five years since Andrew had been elected council president that Ol' Ben could recollect dissension between the two men. It was obvious to Ol' Ben that a power struggle was imminent and on the horizon.

"Poppa. You can't be serious! You know how hard these men have trained. For some of them it's all they know," Caesar said the dread apparent on his face. "I can tell you my men aren't going to take this lying down."

"I don't believe your men have a choice," Jeremiah said staring sadly at his son. "This not a suggestion but an order and as soldiers it is not our job to question but to simply follow orders."

"But I know you father and you are probably as hurt by these orders as anyone. You have spent your life putting this army together. I know for a fact without even asking that you don't want to see something you spent your whole life building torn apart. I know in my heart that you don't want to don't want to throw away your life's work father."

"I don't. But if there's one constant in life it's change. And we have fought the good battle to save our land and to be treated and respected as men. We've gained that. We've gotten to a place where there is no imminent threat or danger and yet our army grows while our schools and hospitals deteriorate."

"Now you are sounding like Uncle Andrew."

"And it is your uncle who holds the deed to this place and made it all possible. He was the one who had the vision to see that with education we could be. And if you look around you will notice that Three Winds is not only thriving but doing better than most of the white plantations in Mississippi. He did that and it wasn't from having superior military might. It was because he had the intellect and vision to see."

Caesar dropped his head.

"That may have been then but this is now. Now we have might and intellect poppa. You can't reign superior without a combination of both."

"You may be right son," Jeremiah said patting the young man on his back, "but for now we must act as good soldiers and follow orders."

"Yes sir and then we will see if we can't persuade Uncle Andrew to see the importance of having a standing army poppa," Caesar said suddenly a smile spreading across his face.

In the meantime Petunia had already gone about employing Joshua and his son's who were all, save one, serving there two years mandatory military service to get a feel from others in the military on how they felt about the cuts in the military.

Joshua arrived at six a.m. that morning.

"Top of the morning to you ma'am. And how are you this morning?" Joshua said as he tied the big gray sorrel to the fence post.

"Another day upright is another day blessed by His goodness Joshua," Petunia said smiling back. "Coffee?"

"No. I'm good. Just stopped by to let you know that according to the boys the overall sentiment seems to be split right down the middle. Seems that a good deal of the men are opposed to Andrew's plan but those are composed of the younger men who don't choose to do anything but police and soldier. Seems that most if not all of the older men that actually stood on the front lines and fought with us and had a chance to actually experience all the bloodshed and all the killing back in the day are all in favor of Andrew's proposal."

"Just as I thought," Petunia replied, a look of worry and concern now showing on her face. "The youngsters don't know. All they can see is the glory of victory. They don't know and can't see the pain and hardship that comes along with it. They can't see the pain and hardship that comes along with it. They can't see the pain on a mother's face or the widow as she stands there in the doorway her babies clutching her apron strings when you have to tell her her son's and husbands won't be coming home again."

Joshua dropped his head. He who had already lost one son knew the pain she spoke of..

"With age comes wisdom."

"That is so true Joshua. What would you propose we do?"

"If I were you I would make sure Andrew attends the next council meeting along with some of the older and more respected men of the council and have them give their accounts and when it's all over let's see who is still gung ho about fighting. Most of these young men were still babies when we were fighting. And when it's over give your account of what it meant to you."

"Thank you Joshua. I think I'll do just that but please not a word to Andrew. I think he has enough on his plate."

"Mum's the word missus. Just glad I was able to help."

"Oh, how rude of me... How are missus and the boy's?"

"They're good. She has me building on an addition to the house and if she finds I snuck away there'll be hell to pay so let me go."

Petunia laughed.

"Tell Candace I got the yellow calico she asked for and I'll bring it down just as soon as I get a chance."

"I'll do that and will keep an ear to the ground and will send one of the boys if there are any new developments."

Petunia stood and hugged the man tightly.

"Thanks Joshua. You have always been a dear friend."

"It is I who should be thanking you. We owe all we have to you and Andrew and the good Lord above. It is I who should be thanking you. Give Andrew my regards and tell him I will see him as soon as I can break away from my new massa. I don't believe things were any harsher when the colonel was in charge," he said wheeling the big sorrel around and galloping off.

Petunia laughed before whisking her petticoats around and heading back indoors. No sooner had she closed the door than she heard the sound of hooves. Opening the door she was surprised to find Ol' Ben just as spry at ninety as he'd been thirty years earlier.

"Morning Missy. Just the person I wanted to see. Where's that young Buck of yours?"

Greeting him she hugged him deeply.

"And what do we owe the honor of this visit? Or should I say Andrew," she laughed. "I know you didn't come to see me."

Ben didn't laugh and Petunia knew that the nature of his visit was something of a serious matter especially at this time of morning.

"Actually I did come to see you and was kind of hoping Andrew wouldn't be here."

Petunia offered Ben a seat on the front porch.

"Or would you prefer to go inside and have a seat in the study Ben. I just find it so nice to sit out here at this time of the morning. It's so cool and peaceful."

"This is fine Petunia," the old man said his demeanor never changing.

"Would you like a cup of coffee Ben?"

"No, I'm fine."

"So what do I owe the honor of this visit? I know it must be serious if you came to see me at this time of morning."

"I believe it is Petunia and I would have brought it to Andrew's attention if it had been about any other topic. But I don't think Andrew would have given me the time of day if I had approached him about dissension in the ranks and especially when it came to his most trusted friend and second in command."

Petunia listened intently now.

"As you probably know the council met last night. Jeremiah led the meeting and addressed the council members around a new agenda. Now you know that I am retired and only act as a consultant when asked to. Last night I just sat and listened. I talked to Andrew about the proposed changes and agree with him wholeheartedly but I'm afraid that the way it was presented wasn't done in a very convincing way. The way it was presented was if I didn't know any better in a most provocative way. It was done in a way that if I didn't know any better I would say would undermine Andrew's entire agenda. And you know as well as I do that Jeremiah is one hell of a leader. And with any good leader he can make his men follow him through the depths of hell if he so chose to."

"And you're telling me this to say what Uncle Ben?"

"I know Jeremiah and Andrew have been friends since childhood but it's a fair assumption to say that Jeremiah may no longer have the best interest of Three Winds at heart. From what I witnessed last night I think that he has an agenda all his own. And that can be a dangerous thing. I just came by to let you know. I could be wrong but I'd keep a watchful eye out. I don't think Andrew would take this coming from anyone but you. I don't mean to cause any problems or cause any dissension but I thought you should know."

Petunia was quiet for a long time after Ben was finished before she spoke.

"Thank you Uncle Ben. And don't feel as though you've done anything wrong. I've had the same feelings myself but I'm like you I don't think Andrew would listen to me anymore than he would you when it came to something concerning Jeremiah. But I sent Joshua to the council meeting last night and he came to me this morning with basically the same story. I don't know what to do accept sit back and wait. I don't think it'll be long 'til Andrew comes to the realization that Jeremiah doesn't have his best interest or the interest of Three Winds at heart. I do so appreciate you coming to me and giving me your take on the whole situation. Without your perception and insight we would never be where we are today. I wish now more than ever that you had succeeded Andrew as head of the council."

Ol' Ben chuckled softly to himself.

"I think that would have been a bit too much for an old geezer like me. But anyway I just rode over here to tell you to watch out for Andrew."

"How did your men take the news?"

"Well, we've kept a standing militia of two hundred and it's always been like that. We need that many to protect the place so the changes don't really affect us and our allegiance has always been with Andrew so…"

"So we can count on your men if it ever gets to that point?"

"You know better than to ask," the old man said shoving a wad of tobacco into his mouth. "Now let me get outta here."

Petunia got up from her favorite rocker walked over to the old man and helped him to his feet and embraced him tightly.

"I love you Uncle Ben."

"I love you too Sissycat," he said before mounting the old brown mule.

Petunia returned to the rocking chair. In the rise to being the sole heir to Three Winds Andrew couldn't have had two more trustworthy lieutenants than Joshua and Ol' Ben. Both men had approached her this morning with the same story which only confirmed her suspicions. But could Jeremiah Andrew's most trusted confidante really be conspiring against him? It was hard to believe but then it wouldn't be the first time that betrayal from those closest to one had occurred in the annals of history.

Still, there wasn't enough evidence to confront Jeremiah on right through her so she set out to confirm that her speculations had been right.

"Jojo," Petunia said. A young man about sixteen or seventeen of spectacular build appeared. Standing a little over six three in his stocking feet, a blacksmith by trade, the young man wore no more than a leather vest and britches his muscles glistened in the morning sun.

"Yes momma?"

"Do me a favor sweetheart. Hitch up Missy Anne and bring my carriage around front please."

"The young man smiled at his mother and within minutes was back with his mother's carriage.

"Need me to drive you momma?" the young man asked. Although she had no favorites the baby who had given her the most pain and turmoil in childbirth was clearly her favorite.

"No, young man I am quite capable of driving myself. Besides I don't want to have to beat one of them little girl's behinds down trying to talk to my handsome young son."

The boy smiled sheepishly.

"And if I'm not mistaken you have a stable full of horses that are need of shodding."

"Okay momma," Jojo said still grinning.

Petunia was off with a flurry. Her thoughts suddenly went from the conceived conspiracy that threatened them all to Jojo. He was the youngest, the one most like Andrew and the one she worried about most. Steadfast and bright as a new day he more than any of her other children most resembled Andrew.

Quiet and handsome he despite being the youngest was the most solemn and peaceful with wisdom far surpassing his older siblings. When they would quarrel over the most mundane of things it was Jojo who would reach a level of compromise that would bring peace once again to the household. Never a harsh word did he say and the room would light up when he walked in. And never no matter how harsh she would chastise him in her never ending tirade she considered parenting in order to make him stronger and tougher for the world he wouldn't do anything other than take it in an easy stride, smile and simply acknowledge with a 'yes momma'. He was the only one of her children who had never set foot in a classroom and she was good with that.

He read incessantly and she feared that formal schooling would do more harm than good. Jojo was a freethinker and any boundaries and parameters put on him she worried would only limit his growth. Andrew argued that he needed the experience of socializing with other children but Petunia countered that the only socialization the boy who stood six feet at the age of twelve with his fine features and good looks would encounter would be between the legs of some young girl or woman in need of getting her itched scratched. Petunia won this argument and she watched as he progressed and only offered minor direction in his case.

A half an hour later, Petunia approached Fiona's home. It loomed large in the distance and appeared even larger as she approached. The white picket fence was freshly painted and the roses which travelled up the trellis to the veranda were absolutely gorgeous. Petunia smiled as she recollected on how far they had come from Missy Anne's kitchen.

Fiona had been her best friend all of her life. Knocking on the front door Petunia thought of the big house they called Magnolia and wondered what Missy Anne would have said if she could see Fiona now.

"Hey honey," Fiona said seeing Petunia and giving her a hug. "I was just thinking about you?"

"Good thoughts I hope."

"Always. Come on in." Fiona led her friend past the spacious living room and the spiral staircase into the kitchen.

"Remember when we used to dream of living in a big house like Magnolia and here you are and we're still in the kitchen," Petunia laughed.

Fiona smiled.

"Old habits die hard," Fiona replied still smiling.

"Were you on your way out?"

"Nowhere but to the hospital. Since Andrew opened it up to all the niggras in Jackson County we can't keep up. Its okay but and I understand but Lord knows I can't wait 'til we get the new hospital built and we get some more staff. Right now we're overwhelmed."

Petunia knew right then and there from her friend's remarks that Fiona was still on board.

"From what I hear Jeremiah made it known to the council that the military would be cut in order to fund the hospital and schools. You know we ain't got nearly enough schools."

"Don't I know."

"Here's the thing Fi-. Jeremiah made the announcement knowing full well that there would be some resentment and did nothing to quell the disturbance and you know if he was in earnest and made a plea for the schools and the hospital he could have easily change the minds of those men. They look at him like he's a god."

"Is that so is it? Funny you bring that up because he always comes home and we talk about what happened at the meetings and last night I thought it strange when he simply said 'nothing of importance' and rolled over and went to sleep. He knows how important my work at the hospital is and what it means to me. And you're telling me he didn't even fight for the hospital. Now that I think of it Caesar didn't mention it either. He done lost his damn mind."

"I'm not trying to stir up a hornets' nest Fi-. It's bad enough there are rumors of that ol' crazy woman that beat one daughter with a cast iron skillet and tied another of her daughter's to a tree and whipped her paddy roller style. Soon as I heard it I knew it couldn't be anyone but your crazy ass."

"Yeah P. something like that but you know I don't tolerate no crazy shit. He done let that there council president shit go to his head but he gonna hear from the first lady tonight when I get home you can best believe that. Come on and give me a hand down at the hospital. You know we short staffed. And thinking of it why ain't you down at the school house today?"

"It's Saturday Fi-."

"Lord I've been working so hard I've lost track of the days. Still, from the younguns I've seen running 'round here lately these niggras don't ever need a day off."

Petunia laughed before the two women hugged and went their separate ways.

She felt relieved knowing that Fiona would never waver when it came to her principles and was glad Fiona still remained her oldest and dearest friend.

Chapter 2

There was no reason training should stop and Caesar pushed his men like any other day. The sweat glistened off the black skin of the thirty or so Black men in the hot Mississippi sun as Caesar barked command after command before realizing the scorching sun right overhead screamed it was midday.

"At ease gentleman. We had a good workout today but before you go I'd like to say a few words. First of all, we were all there last night and heard that there would be cuts made to the military. As you all know those cuts won't affect us in any way but they will affect our brothers and if you train as hard as we do then I know you're vested in this thing of ours. Those men in the regular militia may not be so blessed as to join our elite special force but they are also vested. They have a certain value and I believe their worth is being taken for granted in the name of progress. We have become too soft, too comfortable. Too many of us believe that because we have not seen the enemy in some time then that enemy does not exist. The enemy does exist and the minute he gets word of us relaxing our defenses he will be on us to subdue us and take control once more. But I have a proposal that I think will show our worth as well put a little change in our britches. All of you that may have some interest please stay for a few and I will detail my plans."

As many of the young men had been Caesar's boyhood friends they stayed to listen as a new leader was emerging.

That night the sky shone brightly as the moon illuminated the evening sky and the men assembled at the northern most part of Three Winds. On horses there stood twelve of Three Winds elite group of guerilla soldiers dressed in all black with black masks covering their faces.

"We all know the plan. We're well trained and proficient at what we do. Our goal is to get in and out with little or no bloodshed. We hit 'em quick, hard, fast and we're out. Does everyone understand?"

Eager to get underway the young men nodded in agreement before Caesar tugged hard on the reins of the big bay wheeling her around and galloping off in the direction of Jackson eleven of his chosen men at his heels.

The men rode hard that night and forty five minutes later they reached Jackson's perimeter where they split into two teams. The first team made up of Caesar and some of his more trusted recruits made their way along the backstreets until they reached the jail. One deputy was on duty manning the sheriff's office when they arrived. Caesar knocked softly at the door to the jail. The deputy who appeared about the same age as Caesar opened the door only to face six armed gunmen and was quickly bound and gagged and locked in the empty jail cell. As quickly as they'd come they were gone.

Once back out on the deserted main street Caesar pulled out a jug of hooch and began sipping it when the second deputy approached.

"What you doing out here boy? You know there ain't no public drinking on the streets. Come on nigga. You're going with me," the old white deputy said never feeling the crashing thud of the gun butt.

"Hurry men. Drag him inside quickly before someone sees." A minute later he too laid bound and gagged while the blood trickled where the gun butt had been. The whole affair had taken no more than ten minutes.

"Let's go. We have other business at hand," Caesar said as he glanced back at the two deputies laying unconscious on the cell floor. Grabbing their horses they headed two blocks down and then up and over to Main Street before crossing over and pulling up in back of the bank where they found the other half of their unit already hard at work inside.

"How are we doing?"

"A few more bags to go," Elijah said.

"Hurry then," Caesar said glancing at his watch. "The rest of you mount up."

A few minutes later all twelve rode at an easy pace towards Three Winds. Still fairly early when they approached Three Winds they hid the money in an already predetermined place in the woods not far from where they trained then dispersed and found their way to their respective homes with little or no words passing between them.

"Caesar what is this I hear of you opposing the council's decision to cut back on the military?"

"Ah ma, all I was saying was that that's all some of the men know is how to be good soldiers. Some of these men have spent twenty or more years defending Three Winds and now all of a sudden you want them to abandon the only thing they know and for what?"

"Trust me son and I believe I know better than you but those men that have been in the military for twenty years were there in the beginning and unlike you know the horrors of warfare. They know what it is to see their son or best friend shot and maimed with a leg or arm hanging off. They know what it's like to go to a friend or neighbor's wife and tell her that her husband won't be coming home that night. All you know is what your father tells you of the glory of the battles we won. But what he fails to tell you is the pain and heartache that came with each victory. The only thing good about those days is that they got us to where we are today. There is no good that can come out of a lifetime of killing."

Caesar was angry now. He loved his mother but times had changed. How long had they been slaves? In his mind one day was too long. They should have organized, trained and been ready to throw the shackles off. But no they'd shuffled at the mercy of a few wealthy southern crackers and allowed themselves to be whipped, hung and emasculated.

Well, times had a changed and no more were Black folk gonna suffer endless indignities at the hands of white folks. No. Now they would be the aggressor and inflict the wrath of free Black men on them. And they were more than ready.

Caesar exited the same way he'd entered. Only now he was angry. Grabbing the reins he pulled tightly causing the horse to rise up and whinny hard. Turning he galloped away.

"Let him go," Fiona said as Jeremiah rose to go after the boy. "It's too late for that now. You should have told him the truth when he first brought the matter to your attention but you were so busy trying to hold onto the little power you have that you let your son and a host of good men cause dissension where there should be none."

Jeremiah dropped his head in shame.

"I only hope you have the nerve and the strength to go to Andrew in the morning and apologize to him for what you have done."

"I will do that," was all the mountain of a man could muster.

Chapter 3

A quarter of a mile away Caesar pulled back hard on the reins as he approached the tiny cottage in the clearing. A small rose garden adorned the front of the house and a small garden sat off to the side.

Knocking softly the shuffle of feet could be heard inside.

"Who is it?" came the sound of a young woman's voice from inside the tiny cottage.

"It's me. Caesar."

Taking the latch off stood a beautiful mulatto woman of no more than nineteen.

"Wasn't expecting you. Mandy must be busy tonight," the young woman said smiling before noticing that something was definitely wrong with the tall, handsome man that stood before her.

"You gonna invite me in or what?"

"What's wrong Caesar? You look like you had a rough one tonight. Wanna tell me about it?"

"It's nothing. Just had an argument with momma is all."

"Well, you should know better than to tangle with her. She's been through a lot more wars than you have. She also has the wisdom of time on her side."

"That may be all well and good but the bottom line is that time's are a changing and I don't think she's really in touch with where we are today and what we're capable of as a people. We're not slaves anymore and the sky's the limit. Instead of sitting back we need to step forward and demand what's rightfully ours. After all we're the ones that built this country. And we have the superior numbers. But Black folks get a little taste of freedom and now they just content to sit back and take the leftovers and scraps tossed their way. If you ask me ain't much difference between now and slavery."

The woman sat back and listened intently without interrupting. When he was finished she handed him a glass of elderberry wine.

"Do you feel me Celeste? Don't you think it's time for Black folks to forget slavery and take the bull by the horns and take what is rightfully ours?"

The young woman who appeared to be considerably younger than Caesar sipped her wine casually seemingly in no rush to give Caesar an answer. When she finally did speak she chose her words carefully.

"You remind me of another niggra fellow with similar ideas. He too saw the world not as it was but as it should be and he like you was gonna make a difference. I believe his name was Nat Turner. And though I admire him I have to wonder if he couldn't have made more of an impact if he had lived."

"Nat Turner was not organized, didn't have the best trained troops at his disposal and had no plan other than a vision he had from God."

"He was not ready and neither are you Caesar. You may have all the drive and desire needed but you have to temper your enthusiasm and channel your bitterness into something more positive other than and trying to go to war against white folks. And in so doing you will be able to see more clearly and make more of an impact. Do you know why our parents were so successful? They were successful because they plotted a course of action that would better themselves as a people and in so doing have created one of the greatest southern plantations one has ever known Black or white."

"But we can be better," Caesar said now pleading his case.

"That we can be. But what is it that my pappy used to tell me? All things in time."

"Who has time Celeste? We can't just sit back and wait for things to happen. We have to make things happen if we want them to be."

"And how do you propose to do that my love?"

"Do you love me Celeste?"

"I think you know the answer to that my love."

"And you have promised to marry me?"

"I have."

"And at the rate we're going how long do you think it'll be before that happens?"

"Well, with me saving the little I get teaching and you in the army maybe two or three years."

"My argument exactly. At the rate we're going we'll be old and gray before we're able to have children of our own."

"Patience is a virtue Caesar. God has a plan. And you can't rush the Lord's hand."

"Tonight we did. That's what I'm telling you. We can't continue to be reactive. We have to be proactive and make things happen. I know the Lord helps those who help themselves but the Lord is a busy man and sometimes he needs us to step up. That's what we did tonight."

"Who is we and what did you do Caesar?"

"Me, Buck and a few of the other fellas went in to Jackson and robbed the bank," the young man said smiling.

"*No you didn't,*" Celeste shrieked aloud.

"Yes, but no one was hurt and a rough estimate says we made off with close to forty thousand dollars."

Ignoring the amount Celeste screamed.

"Caesar Augustus! What in heaven's name is wrong with you? You're going to have every poor white cracker from Jackson to Natchez looking at Three Winds for the niggras that did it."

"And we'll be ready. The federal government is the only army in the United States with a larger army than we have right here. And we have the finest regiment of guerilla soldiers in the world so let them come. And when they come then folks like my mother who are content and think that we've finally arrived we'll see the importance of having a standing army."

"Do you hear what you're saying Caesar? You're willing to risk the lives of every man, woman, boy and girl so you can say that Three Winds has a strong army. God help you if anything befalls Three Winds because of your arrogance. Caesar I think it's time for you to go," she said standing and holding the front door open.

Caesar left disheartened. If anyone would understand he was sure Celeste would. After all she'd suffered through a slavery he'd never known. She if anybody should have been elated at the idea of armed retribution but she like momma and all the rest were pacifists but despite his love for his mother and Celeste this was a mission he was called to ride out and that he would do despite the naysayers. They would ultimately thank him in the end.

When the dew hit along with the chilly morning air Caesar awoke. Cold and damp he rose from between the two Sycamore trees walked out of the woods and made his way home his horse in tow.

The oldest of eight it was easy to get lost in the shuffle and Caesar did just that hoping not to run into his mother. Eager to get busy Caesar grabbed a fresh change of clothes along with a clean uniform and headed down the long stairs and out the back door. It would be the last time he would enter his parent's home. Stopping by his uncle's he asked his aunt if she could write him a bank note so he wouldn't have to ride into Natchez with such a large sum of money.

Petunia was used to doing this for the residents of Three Winds and thought nothing of it. And after all, Caesar was a good boy.

It was too soon after the robbery to go into Jackson but time was a wasting and so with a draft for a little over a thousand dollars Caesar Augustus drove the painted bay into Natchez where he proceeded to head to the lumber yard and purchase the materials needed for his new home. By nightfall he was back at Three Winds but unlike the night before did not disclose the details of his visit to Jackson when he rode up to Mandy's house on the hill.

Mandy the cute, diminutive wife of his best friend and second lieutenant Buck was brown skinned and standing less than five feet tall, Mandy was a little fireball always going on about this or that. Buck's pride and joy she was Caesar's comic relief when Buck wasn't around. And since Buck was covering as a favor for Caesar today and tomorrow while Caesar handled some personal business why not stop and see Mandy.

Entering the house Caesar grabbed Mandy by the waist and pulled him tightly to him before kissing her deeply, passionately. The tiny woman did not object to his advances and instead welcomed them openly melting into his caress. Then with little or no effort Caesar lifted her from the floor. The pretty young woman let her dress fall to the floor before wrapping her legs around his waist. Unbuckling his belt and letting his pants drop to the floor he entered her deeply causing her to gasp as she wrapped both her arms around his neck. Lifting her up one hand grabbing the cheeks of her buttocks he raised her up and then let her fall taking the shaft of his penis deep inside her. And each time she let out a shriek that could be heard in the deepest recesses of the galaxy followed by a chorus of...

"Oh daddy! That's the spot daddy. Right there! It feels so good when you fuck my tight, little pussy. Oh yes daddy!"

Moments later, both spent and exhausted the two collapsed onto the sofa below.

"You gettin' better every time I see you girl."

"What can I say? I learned from the best," she grinned.

Mandy was a pretty mulatto gal with skin the color of coffee with a tad too much cream. Born of a French singer in New Orleans, her daddy boasted African roots and Mandy bore certain African features that only endeared her to the men of Three Winds. With a tiny waist that exploded into thunderous thighs and a perfectly round ass she enamored herself to all. But there was only one man that she saw at Three Winds and that was Caesar. From the time of her arrival to the large plantation then owned by the colonel she had set her eyes on Caesar although she was five years his junior.

After repeatedly turning down her proposals for marriage she'd married his best friend to spite him. Yet, despite the marriage to Buck she remained in love with Caesar and he in some way with her. But before anything else could transpire he had to keep up appearances for Buck.

"Was wondering if I could use the guest room for a few days. If you coming to me like that I'd be an absolute fool to say no."

Caesar smiled.

"You can use the guest room forever as long as you keep giving it to me like that daddy," she said smiling.

Caesar winked as he buttoned his trousers and headed for the door.

"I'll be back. Gotta get Buck's permission," Caesar said winking at the very attractive young woman in front of him.

Riding out on the bluff overlooking the valley below he saw his men training. He considered himself a task master but he was easy in comparison to Buck who would train and drill the men from six am to eight or nine at night. Caesar eased the big bay down the ravine to the edge. Seeing Caesar Buck gave the soldiers a much needed break before heading over to his friend.

"How'd it go today?"

"Good. Rode up to Natchez and ordered supplies so I can get started on that house I always wanted. Now I can ask Celeste to marry me. So, my friend I would say all-in-all it was a good day. I need a favor though."

"Anything for you my friend."

"I need a place to rest my head for a few days. Momma and I went at it pretty bad last night so I went to Celeste's and didn't fare much better."

"You know that's not a problem. Just explain the situation to Mandy or she may look at you sideways."

"Thanks my brother. I'll see what she says. And let the men know that in two days we go again. Natchez this time so tell them to rest up."

Buck's eyes lit up.

"That's what I'm talking about. I think it's time Mandy and I start thinking about a family."

"That's the spirit my friend. I'll be here to relieve you at this time tomorrow night. Oh, and Buck whatever you do don't kill the men before we take Natchez." Caesar laughed.

"I'll try not to," Buck laughed.

Caesar rode off. It was getting dark now and he considered riding up to Celeste's and apologizing but the days were getting shorter and he still had work to do. The first course of action was Mandy.

Chapter 4

"Morning Andrew," said the tall man who sat high in the saddle.

"Morning sheriff. What brings you out to Three Winds this morning? Could it be the view? I was just admiring it myself," Andrew said looking out over the sprawling breathtaking view that was Three Winds.

"It is beautiful Andrew but that's not why I came out here this morning. You see the bank was robbed two nights ago and two of my deputies were beaten and gagged. Said a niggra set them up. I was just wondering if you'd heard anything?"

"I sure haven't sheriff. This is the first I'm hearing about it but you know it wasn't any of the niggras here at Three Winds."

"I know that Andrew but I've run out of leads and well if you have to know this was my last stop because I've exhausted all other leads. But when they said that the niggras that did this were both disciplined and well trained I naturally thought of your people."

"I guess that's some sort of backwards compliment and I acknowledge you for that but I can assure you it wasn't anyone from here. You know there are some other intelligent niggras besides us."

"Touche," the sheriff said before wheeling his horse around and leaving at a gallop. "Good day Andrew."

"What was that all about?" Petunia said as she came out to sweep the porch.

"Sheriff just came out to pay us a compliment sweetiepie."

"Is that all Andrew?"

"That's all," Andrew repeated.

A rider was approaching. There was no mistaking the big man in the saddle. Jeremiah jumped off the big red sorrel with the quickness of a twenty year old. Andrew broke into grin that covered his entire face.

"What's the occasion my friend? Is it a holiday? Fiona let you out?"

"Yeah, now let's see if you can get a day away from your ova'seer," Jeremiah replied grinning just as broadly. "Where's your fishing gear?"

"In the back in the shed," Andrew replied.

"Well, grab it man. I'll keep Petunia busy while you get it and head out the back. I'll meet you down by the creek."

"I wish I could but I'm up to my neck in work and the old lady has me working on getting the new schools up and running. I'm starting to actually think it was easier under the colonel. Ya' gotta be careful what you wish for." The two men laughed and hugged each other.

"Let's have a seat on the porch my brother."

"I am fine on this old stump," Jeremiah replied. "Besides I cannot stay long. I too have work to do. But first there is a matter of the utmost importance which I must address with you."

Andrew knew Jeremiah all too well and knew that there was something troubling him.

"Yes. Go ahead. Tell me what is troubling you."

Jeremiah recounted the council meeting and how he had not actively supported Andrew's proposal.

"Call it ego. Call it the intoxication of power. Whatever it was I was lost. I became what it is I most loathe. I am so thankful Fi- is in my life. She saw the error of my ways and addressed it as only she can. She shamed me into coming here this morning and I'm glad she did. I apologize my friend for being selfish and disloyal but I believe we have a bigger problem at hand."

"I already knew but I had faith in my friend and whether Fiona was there or not you would have come to me sooner or later. After all we are brothers."

"There is something else that gravely concerns me though Andrew."

"And what is that Jeremiah?"

"Well, when I spoke to everyone at the council meeting the men were clearly disturbed. But I think Caesar took it hardest. I tried to explain to him that it wouldn't be his unit but he's adamant about the army staying intact."

"He's young. He'll be okay."

"No, Andrew. They are not the same as we were. These boys are angry. They're bitter. They're well trained, the best we have by far and they're itching for a confrontation and I don't think it matters much if the confrontation comes from within or without."

"That serious huh?"

"I hate to say it but I think so. After Fi- tore into me she went after Caesar. He took offense to it and stormed out. He hasn't returned since that night. He said he had a plan. And with his youth and recklessness he could be dangerous."

"Yes. He could prove dangerous but what it comes down to is youth and age. And I would hardly bet against age and experience."

"I hope you're right my friend."

"You and me both but first I'd like to speak with him. Do you think you could arrange that?"

"I will certainly try."

Chapter 5

Caesar spent most of the day he was in Natchez ordering materials for his new home casing the bank and telegraph office. The city which was no more than a big town posed some dilemmas but in the following days he'd come up with a plan. A three pronged attack was needed to insure everyone's safety. The first part would be a diversionary attack to summon the authorities. Then there was the job of cutting the telegraph wires so there would be no communication with outside authorities. And then there was the whole matter of the bank which was no more fortified than the bank in Jackson.

Once he had the plan in hand he went over the plan with his lieutenants. A day later they set off in three sets of five.

Reaching Natchez early in the evening they stopped off in the bottoms to Ol' Miss Avery's liquor and whore house for a drink and to look over the plan for the final time. Buck took the first unit out to the easternmost part of the city limits while Caesar waited.

The telegraph office was also on the eastern end of the city while the bank and their escape route were at the west end. Caesar and the others waited until they saw the signal. Once they saw the billowing smoke they mounted up and headed for the bank. Reaching the rear of the bank they heard the alarm and watched as every one of the good citizens of Natchez raced to lend a hand at the fire. This was just as Caesar had planned it.

The bank itself was quite a bit harder than he could have expected with the vault having reinforced doors. Luckily they'd brought the dynamite for the telegraph office and the four sticks proved enough to blast a whole in the door to the vault. With everyone preoccupied at the far end of town no one heard the thunderous explosion at the other end of town.

A day later, Buck pulled Caesar to the side.

"What did we do on that last job?"

"A little over eighty grand."

Buck's eyes lit up.

"Goodness! We could actually retire off of just that one haul."

"We could. But I have some bigger things on the burner. Just hang in there and trust me."

The next week the news of the bank hold up was all anyone was talking about. The newspapers attributed the bank hold ups to professionals and more importantly northern agitators now stealing what poor southerners had left following the war.

There was nothing however that linked the men responsible for the bank hold ups which pleased Caesar and Buck for the time being. The raids continued with Caesar and his men becoming more and more brazen in their attacks and not limiting their raids to any one portion of the state but travelling to wherever the take seemed largest. Every now and then they'd cross the state line into Alabama and take down a bank or hold up a railroad and in the whole time they prided themselves on the fact that there had never been a casualty.

Oh, there had been some close calls like the day they hit three banks in one day on the way back from Grenada and the posse caught up with them right after they hit the bank in Meridian. All were fine horsemen and on the thoroughbreds now being bred on Three Winds there was little chance of any posse catching them. By this time, the unit had amassed close to three quarters of a million dollars though no one would never have known it. These were disciplined soldiers who ran their raids and robberies like a well oiled machine. But never once had they broken their vow of silence.

"You know when we started out it was in reaction to General Jeremiah's plan to cut the military. It was my understanding that we were to entice the white folks to attack us at Three Winds and in retaliation we would show the general and everyone else who saw the army as disposable that we were an integral part of Three Winds but now we're just robbing and stealing as if that's the end in itself."

"Weren't you the one that told me in the beginning that with our first bank job that you could now get started on a family with Mandy?"

"Yes, my friend but that was then. It's six months later and if we were to stop now Mandy and I could live the remainder of our days quite comfortably and our children's children would never want for anything. So my question to you is why we keep robbing and stealing. When is enough enough?"

"What are you saying my friend?"

"We are already wealthy men Caesar. Greed and avarice will be our downfall. Why not stop and be content with counting our blessings."

"Because that is not who we are. This is not what we do. We are good men who believe in God the Father and his teachings. And we who have been persecuted and ridiculed for the color of our skin should be the last ones persecuting others. Remember that the first shall be last and the last shall be first. That is how we were raised and who we are Caesar."

"I cannot condemn any man his faith and least of all you my brother nor will I try to convince you to abandon your faith and continue to ride with us but I am curious to know as my second lieutenant how you would proceed from here."

"Cease these senseless raids before someone is killed Caesar. Forget if you have not already forgotten what our initial goal was. Do not unmask yourselves. If you were to unmask yourself we would not have a chance. We'd have the entire state of Mississippi upon us for all the crimes we've committed."

Caesar hung his head in shame. Few people could speak to him in such a manner but Buck was one of the few that could.

"If provocation is still your means of persuading your uncle and your father that a standing army is necessary then I suggest you wait six months to a year my friend until everything cools down to a simmer before lashing out again."

"I respect your opinion and will give it considerable thought Buck and I pray that whatever decision I make it in no way affects our friendship."

"We are not boys anymore Caesar. We are men and as men we owe each other the truth no matter how hard it is."

"This is true."

"Come on. I'm sure Mandy has dinner waiting for us," Buck said throwing the hammer into the toolbox.

They'd been working on Caesar's house for close to three months now and it was nearly completed. And a fine house it was. Still, without Celeste this house would never be the home he dreamed of. She had hardly spoken to him since that night. He'd gone by on several occasions to try to explain and apologize but she like Buck was not in concert with his current activities. There were even rumors out that his cousin Jojo was courting Celeste. He dispelled this knowing that she'd already promised her hand to him.

Buck kissed his wife gently on the cheek but Mandy's eyes were clearly focused on the man who now stood behind her husband.

"Evening Mandy," Caesar said as he passed the two on his way up the stairs.

"Going to bed without dinner?"

"Yes I am. I'm beat. You two have a good evening," Caesar said barely above a whisper. Mandy turned and looked at Buck.

"He's had a rough day. Nothing to be worried about sweetheart," Buck said turning and kissing his wife on the forehead.

"Celeste?" Mandy asked.

"Among other things," Buck said heading towards the table where his dinner awaited.

Chapter 6

The next morning was a scorcher and the Mississippi sun helped little. Only the west end of the porch needed to be completed and Caesar was committed to having that done by noon when a lone rider pulled up.

"Morning Uncle Andrew," Caesar said grinning widely. He'd always had a particular affinity for this man who stood so tall in the saddle and carried an air of dignity about him. He was regal and what the African kings must have resembled in Caesar's mind. "What brings you out this way this morning?"

"It's a funny thing. I keep hearing all these wonderful things about my favorite nephew and I realized that I haven't taken the time to ride out and tell him how proud I am of him. So, I told your auntie before I went to sleep last night that the first thing I 'm going to do in the morning was to ride out and see you although with my back and all I do wish you'd move closer instead of so far away."

"I'm glad you did. So what do you think uncle?"

"It's as I was told; a fine house. You can raise a family here."

"Yes those are my intentions if I can ever get this woman to come around."

"And by that woman I can assume you're talking about Celeste."

"Yes."

"And I guess you know she and Jojo have been courting rather heavily."

"Yes I'm aware of that."

"And this does not worry you?"

"I have no time to worry about what others do. I can only concentrate on what it is that I have to do to be the best that I can be and if that is not good enough what else can I do?"

"That's a very mature attitude and one that will take you far. Jojo is your favorite cousin. I can remember you as small boys. Oh, how you two loved each other. I understand how choices that we make for ourselves can lead you into different directions as you grow older and become men but whatever you do don't ever forget the love you two shared. And whatever you do don't let a woman come between and separate you."

"Never would I let that happen uncle. I have always believed that you cannot possess another person. If that is the choice Celeste makes then who am I to try to make her choose otherwise."

"You are so right. A woman is funny and I don't profess to know any more in all my years than you do young man. If I have learned anything it's that you learn more by watching and listening and getting to know them as much as you can before trying to understand a woman.

Are you still reading and keeping up with current events?"

"I try uncle. Haven't really been able to as much as I'd like to with the house and work and all."

"I know you've heard about the recent rash of robberies and hold ups?"

"Yeah, that's really something isn't? Say they're pretty professional and disciplined."

"And Black."

"Get out of here. You mean to tell me that these are Black folks pulling off those robberies? That's hard to believe."

"Well, they don't know for sure. You know when they held the first bank up in Jackson the sheriff came here to see if I knew anything. Of course I didn't but he had to check. I told him that no one on Three Winds would even consider such a thing and when I really gave it some thought I still came to the same conclusion. No one here is so selfish that they would jeopardize the whole of us for a few dollars."

"I don't believe any of us here at Three Winds would do anything so foolish as to jeopardize us all."

"I certainly hope not but it is reason for concern."

"I am only glad that I only have to deal with the small issues not the running of something so large as Three Winds."

"It is no easy task but from the good things I've heard you are a prime candidate for the position. If you temper your movements it should be a relatively smooth transition. I hear you are both a fine leader and have a thirst for knowledge that will only help to elevate the status of Three Winds and its niggras. Just go slow my nephew and remember 'all things in time."

"I will do that Uncle Andrew," Caesar said still grinning.

When his uncle had gone Caesar sat on a hollow log in the front yard and took out a chew of tobacco. In only a matter of hours how many times had he heard the same thing? Was this a matter of coincidence or was God sending him a sign? Whatever it was it was coming from too many different directions but the message was clear.

Uncle Andrew was truly a surprise and it was if he had not only surmised what he was into but warned him about any further infractions. It was as if he knew. But then how could he? The last two days had unnerved him so that after careful deliberation Caesar made it a point to go to his parents that evening and let him know of his decision.

"After having thought about what you said the last time we talked momma I have to agree with you. You brought me up in the church and nowhere in His teachings does it say that one should foster the idea of devoting one's life to taking another and I guess that's what I've done. So, after some careful thought and some soul seeking I want to resign my position as first lieutenant in this man's army," Caesar said now looking into his father's eyes as his own welled up with tears.

Jeremiah grabbed his son and held him tightly and Fiona wrapped her arms around both of them so glad was she to have her son home once again.

"There's a council meeting tonight. I'm going to need you to be there to tell your men of your decision. I don't want there to be any speculatin' or signifyin' as to what prompted you to come up with this decision. In fact, I want you to tell them just as you've told me. This may help me in the long run. Perhaps when the men see the greatest soldier of their time bow out because of his religious and moral convictions perhaps they will see the light as well. I am proud of you son," Jeremiah said hugging his eldest son again."

"So what will you do now," Fiona asked not looking up from the buns she was fixing to put in the oven.

"I'm going back to school and learn a trade. Maybe blacksmithing… And I'd thought I'd start with a few horses and see if I can breed them and grow some tobacco."

"Where will you get the start up money for seed and the horses?" Fiona questioned.

"I have a few dollars saved up and I figured I'd ask Uncle Andrew if he would stake me for the rest until I'm up and running. You know he stopped by today and gave me some advice and some words of encouragement and based on what he said I'm pretty sure he'll do it."

"Well, you couldn't have asked for a better mentor. Let me know how that turns out and don't be a stranger young man. No matter what happens you know your father loves you and worries about you."

"I know momma," Caesar said hugging both of his parents before making his leave. "I'll see you tonight poppa."

For the first time in quite some time Caesar felt good about himself and decided to stop by and grab Buck and tell him of his recent decision. Arriving he found only Mandy.

"If you're looking for your boy he left about twenty minutes ago. He may have gone by your place. He said he had something he needed to run by you. And that reminds me Caesar I have something to show you as well.

Caesar stepped down off the horse and followed the diminutive woman into the house and up the long and winding staircase to the guest room that he used to sleep in. Kneeling before him she unbuckled his trousers.

Chapter 7

The meeting was like any other meeting. Well, it was like any other meeting until Caesar made his speech. Ten years he'd spent in the army but because of the need for schools, the hospital, and the library he would be stepping down so that these concessions could be had. It was a stirring speech complete with the fact that his religion did not train him to kill and when it was over others followed and resigned as well. Now all that was to be done was to name a successor and he did naming Buck the new head of the elite unit he had once coveted.

The days and month passed and Three Winds continued to thrive as it always had with each family striving to better themselves with the good of the community being first on the minds of everyone. They were receiving recognition now as the first niggra town to thrive of its own accord. Schools and hospitals flew up and an extension was added to the now famous Magnolia library. It was now touted as one of the best and most exclusive libraries in the state holding close to fifty thousand volumes. Yes, the niggras at Three Winds had erected something unique, something great while still being ostracized by the larger white community but this was of little or no concern to the residents of Three Winds.

Caesar, for one was in a world of his own. Uncle Andrew had done as he'd promised but instead of giving Caesar the three stallions and six mares he'd doubled that number. Now in less than a year he'd manage to pay his uncle the loan back in full and doubled the number of the herd and predicted that in another two or three years or so he would have almost as many horses as Uncle Andrew. And although he had yet to convince Celeste he'd changed all was good.

Well, all was good until early that morning when Mandy rode up.

"Caesar we need to talk," she said the tears rolling down her cheeks in streams and then rivers as he helped her down off of his horse.

"What's wrong Mandy? Is it Buck?"

"No Caesar. It's not Buck."

"Then what is it sweetie?"

"It's it's," she stuttered. "Oh Caesar I'm pregnant."

"And you're crying? Have you told Buck? My goodness that's all he talks about is you two starting a family."

"Caesar. Buck hasn't been able to have sex since he fell off that horse two months ago. The baby isn't his. It's yours."

Caesar sat down on the porch unable to talk. His mind raced. It couldn't be. It just couldn't. Speechless he sat there trying to sort it out.

"My God gal! What have you gotten us into now?"

"Don't you dare blame me. You had as much to do with this as I did," she was becoming hysterical now.

"I'm sorry Mandy. You're right. This is no time to blame each other. What we need to do is to see what we can do to fix this. Look what I want you to do is go see my mother at the hospital and tell her you need a wee bit of laudanum. Then I want you to go home and mix the laudanum with some hooch and get Buck to drink it. When you feel him getting a little woozy I want you to seduce him. Once you have him going fix him another drink the same way. Convince him that he made love to you and when he wakes up compliment on just how fabulous he was. You've got to convince him that he was the best thing since slice bread in the morning. It's just that easy. No need for panic."

"Or we could end this charade and you approach him face-to-face-; man-to-man and tell him that we've always loved each other and we are going to leave and go away so as not to cause him any more pain and heartache. We could leave and have and raise our own child the way he should be."

"You know I care about you deeply Mandy but I've just started to carve out a place here at Three Winds. All my family is here and for the first time I feel like I belong. Now you want me to uproot everything I've worked so hard for and disgrace myself and my family by leaving with my best friend's wife."

"Oh, but you weren't disgracing yourself when you were fucking your best friend's wife every chance you got."

"You're upset Mandy. Why don't we discuss this when you're in a better state of mind?"

"I bet if it were Celeste you would have your bags packed by now."

"Perhaps but then you're no Celeste."

"I can't believe you said that to me."

"And I can't believe that you thought this whole scenario would end any other way than how it has. You knew there was no happy ending to this love triangle when you set out but you chose to anyway so don't start crying now. It is what it is. Now git on home and start being the wife you never were and tell your husband that you're

pregnant with his child and don't come 'round here no more."

Caesar meant what he said and lifted Mandy into the saddle and slapped the little

red roan on its hind parts sending him scurrying down the road just as it had come in.

Chapter 8

The days were becoming cooler and now the night air had a sort of chill that said the seasons were changing and fall was fast approaching. Jeremiah passed Andrew a plug of tobacco while Petunia sat with a shawl around her on the porch swing crocheting.

"I'm afraid it has been quiet a bit too long?"

"What do you mean," Jeremiah asked puzzled by this latest admission.

"I don't know. Just a premonition I guess but do me a favor and double the guard from here on out."

"You worry too much," mused Jeremiah.

"I keep telling him his tongue is a sword," Petunia added. "Andrew is one of those people that simply can't relax."

"And you two are simply too relaxed if you ask me," Andrew said throwing the chew of tobacco into the grass before storming into the house.

"Don't know what that was about but I'll leave that for you to find out," Jeremiah said before making his way to his horse and bidding Petunia a goodnight.

"What the hell is wrong with you Andrew? That's no way to treat our guests," Petunia yelled.

"Perhaps if you'd been with me and seen how lax the men are out there on patrol you'd understand. And whose job is the security of Three Winds? Jeremiah's and only Jeremiah's. And he's not doing it. He may have the most important job on the place and if he fails to do it he puts all in jeopardy."

"And you told him this in no uncertain words or did you just get up and storm off? He knows no more now than before he came."

"I will speak to him tomorrow and then I will see about having someone else train and employ the troops."

"If that's what your heart tells you to do," Petunia said before sliding under the covers and closing her eyes.

The following day came at a slow steady pace and Andrew for one was glad. He often had premonitions and all too often they proved true. But he'd slept peacefully and was up with the roosters as he was every morning.

"I'm going to ride down and see Jeremiah, P."

"That's still bothering you Andrew?"

"Just something I need to handle. The safety of Three Winds has never been more paramount."

"Handle your business Andrew and give Fi- my regards."

Andrew turned the big bay sharply and trotted off towards the lower forty. Twenty minutes later he pulled up in front of Jeremiah's where Fiona stood on the side of the house scrubbing clothes.

"Morning Fi-. P. sent you a message but for the life of me I can't recall what it was. Might want to ride up to the house and see what she wants."

"P. don't want nothin' and if she did she'd ride down here and tell me. She knows better than to send word by the likes of you. By the time I got it from you it would be all twisted and convoluted that you'd have me going east when I should be going west. No.

She wouldn't hardly send no messages by the likes of you. Now what you up to? You just trying to get Jeremiah to go with you on one of your ol' crazy excursions."

Andrew had to grin. Out of all the people he knew no one knew him better than the one who stood before him.

"Don't make this harder than it has to be. I need the old man for about an hour or so is all. Think a little fishing would be a good place to talk about his retirement."

Fiona burst out laughing.

"Are you kidding me? You nor Jeremiah were built that way? There is no stop or slow down in either of you."

"Seriously Fi-. I think Jeremiah's wisdom and know how could be used better at other things around Three Winds."

"And just how could I better service Three Winds my friend?" Jeremiah said as he leaned against the house content to smile and pack his pipe.

Surprised to find Jeremiah standing there he continued.

"We have several sites under construction and I need an experienced carpenter and foreman to lead these crews in the construction. Have you seen the remodeled general store? It's not fit to be opened and has to be torn down and rebuilt. That's nothing more than a waste of man hours and materials and we don't have enough of either. I need you to draw up the plans and see that they're implemented correctly. That's what we need most right now."

"And who would run the council and security for Three Winds?"

"Split the council head with Ol' Ben. This would be a great honor to him and turn security over to Caesar."

"Caesar?" Fiona shouted.

"And why not? He was a hell of a fine soldier and has proven leadership qualities. And he has the passion and drive to stay on top of things."

"What do you know of his leadership qualities? What has he ever had the occasion to lead?"

Andrew paused before walking over to the large gray stallion and pulled the corn cob pipe out of the saddle bags before pulling out a number of newspaper articles.

Giving each a handful, Andrew sat down on the hollow oak and waited while they perused with interest. When they'd finished they both turned to Andrew.

"I read most of these along the time they were happening. It's been quiet for a few months now though almost as if they just stopped and disappeared into thin air."

"Not into thin air just back to Three Winds," Andrew said smiling as he watched the bewilderment pass first from Fiona's face and then as it settled in on Jeremiah's. "As I was saying the boy has proven leadership qualities."

"Oh my! Are you trying to tell me that you think Caesar is responsible for these armed holdups and bank robberies? Tell me that's not what you're suggesting Andrew?"

"When the first bank hold up in Jackson happened last year the sheriff came to me telling me one of the bank robberies was a niggra I denied any knowledge because I didn't know. But after putting it all together it made sense and if you pay attention to what's going on on Three Winds you'll notice that the new homes being erected are being built by members of your special unit. Still, I had no proof but last week it was confirmed. So, to answer your question, yes I think the boy has great leadership qualities," Andrew grinned.

"I can't believe that fool took that type of risk. He could have gotten himself killed. He could have gotten us all killed," Jeremiah said angrily.

Clearly shaken a smile grew on Fiona's face.

"You two were no different when you were his age. You feared no danger."

Jeremiah began to smile now.

"Youth."

"Like I said there hasn't been a bank robbery in close to a year and I think something scared him off. Well, I spoke to him or maybe he just had a close call. I don't know for sure. Maybe he was just smart enough to call it a day but since then I've had people monitoring his actions and from what I've seen and been told all he's interested in now his ranch and his horses and he's done extremely well at breeding and selling them."

"He's special. I think whatever he puts his mind to he'll be successful at but with this latest news why do you think he'd serve well with our security in his hands?"

"I think it goes back to what you just said. He can be good and effective at whatever path it is that he chooses and if you read the articles closely there were never any casualties on either side. He is if nothing else vigilant and disciplined and puts a value on human life. Do you realize these kids pulled off over a dozen robberies inside the state alone and did not suffer one casualty or inflict harm on anyone else. These robberies were both well planned and well executed. With you and I giving him the needed direction I think he'd make a fairly good leader."

Both Fiona and Jeremiah were still in shock and Andrew's words were taking time to register. When they finally did it was Jeremiah who spoke first.

"I have no doubt that he's capable of what you are asking Andrew. However, what I am more concerned about is his recklessness. Don't you think someone a little older and mature would be a better fit?"

"Probably but with you and I and Ben keeping check I think he'll be fine. And it would free you up from keeping up on them on the daily. There is so much more valuable work you could be doing on behalf of Three Winds."

"I think Andrew's right. Give him the opportunity and the responsibility and I think he can grow into what we all know he can be and with the ranch and the breeding of the horses it won't lead to a lot of free time. And you know what they say; an idle mind is the devil's workshop."

"Well, he certainly won't have any idle time that's for sure," Jeremiah commented still skeptical.

"So, it's agreed?"

Fiona nodded.

"I suppose so," Jeremiah acknowledged knowing that he was outvoted.

"Oh, and Petunia has invited you to the house for dinner tonight. I think I'll invite Caesar as well. It'll be a good chance to tell him what we expect and show our solidarity.

See you at around seven," Andrew said collecting the articles and placing them back in his saddle bag.

The next stop was down to see Caesar. The house had taken on a whole new dimension with its freshly painted shutters and the white picket fence. The young man hearing the horse approaching came out and stood on the front porch. Seeing his uncle he broke into a broad grin.

"And what do I owe the honor? Two visits in less than a month…"

"Just stopped by to invite you to dinner tonight Caesar. We have some pretty important business to discuss. Can we count on you about seven, seven thirty?"

Caesar was puzzled by the invitation but gladly accepted.

Chapter 9

Meanwhile, over in Jackson a small crowd gathered in front of the general store at about the same time Caesar rode in sitting tall and proud. Getting down from the tall thoroughbred he made his way through the crowd and entered the general store.

A man stood atop a soap box ranting and raving. He was able to catch the last few words of the man's speech. He was obviously running for some political office or another but when wasn't there somebody campaigning about this or that. They all made a stop in Jackson being that it was the capitol and boasted being the most populated city in Mississippi. Every politician knew that if you won Jackson's electorate chances were mighty good that you'd win whatever office it was that you were campaigning for so this was nothing unusual for Caesar who'd witnessed this on prior occasions. Still, there was something different about this man's speech.

"The war has been over for quite a spell now and a lot of the good folks of Jackson are still struggling to pay their deeds off. Good folks are losing their homes while the federal government and Northern Yankees are giving land grants to niggas. I tell you I don't know what's going on. It seems like the whole world is turning upside down. They tell me they got niggas right here who own bigger homes than a good deal of the plantations what used to be here. Well, if you good folks want a change and want to go back to when the South was prosperous then we need to get this whole nigga problem solved and take back the land that is rightfully ours as good, southern taxpayers. It was us good white folks of Mississippi built this here land and now we're being swept under the rug by the government, niggas and nigga lovin' Yankees. Well, I say it's time we did something about it and the time is now. And if you vote for me as your next mayor of Jackson and we can begin by taking back what is rightfully ours. Vote for me Clarence Darrow next Tuesday. And whether I am elected your mayor or not I will clean up your nigga problem."

When he finished the crowd erupted in applause. It was all a bit much for Caesar to grasp. What he needed was to get back to Three Winds. Caesar rode out at a steady pace the whole while trying to understand how 'niggas was the problem'.

By the time Caesar reached Three Winds it was already early evening. Going to straight to poppa he was out of breath.

"What's wrong son? Shouldn't you be getting ready for dinner?"

"Poppa, I just left Jackson and they're arming themselves as we speak."

"Is that right?"

"Yes, poppa. There's a man in there goes by the name of Clarence Darrow. Claims he's running for mayor and says he gonna eliminate the nigga problem and return the South to the days of old. He says that Yankees and niggas is the reason the crackers are losing their lands and struggling so."

"Is that so son?"

"Yes, poppa. We'd better double the guard tonight and put them boys on high alert."

"Caesar have you even thought to speak to your mother. Since when did poor white trash supersede good manners?"

"Sorry. Hey momma."

Fiona smiled at her oldest son.

Jeremiah turned and looked at Fiona who was struggling to get her bonnet to sit just right. Turning to look at her husband she smiled.

"How long has Darrow been preachin' hatred Jeremiah?"

"For as long as I can remember but I'm surprised he's runnin' again. The town folk ain't gonna elect him. They saw what happened the last time a Darrow thought he was going to make niggras pay for their troubles."

"Hung his daddy and ended that madness didn't we? Should have hung him too if you ask me."

"If we asked you there wouldn't be no white folk left in Jackson," Jeremiah grinned swinging Fiona up into the air knocking off her bonnet.

"Jeremiah! Look what you done gone and did now," she said smiling and picking her bonnet up off the kitchen floor before addressing her oldest.

"Don't you fret now son. The white folk of Jackson remember the whipping they took the last time they tried to attack Three Winds. There was so much bloodshed and killin' but most if not all was on their side. They don't want no more of that. There may be a few that believe that ol' mess he be saying and he might just 'round up thirty or forty men from 'round the pubs—mostly liquored up poor white trash dirt farmers and try to attack but they ain't no match for the council. And if you'll change clothes and meet us at your uncles I think you'd better understand why them dere crackers don't stand a chance. Now git. You're going to be late."

Caesar was bewildered. He'd just found out and yet they seem to have known all along. It was funny. Despite his stint in the military and preparation they always seem to stay one step ahead of him. It was though God had sent them a sign. What did poppa say? He'd already doubled the guard.

An hour or so later Caesar was greeted at the front door by the first lady of Thee Winds in all her finery.

"Didn't think you were going to make it," Petunia sad kissing Caesar on both cheeks as was the Islamic custom of greeting friends and loved ones.

"Sorry I'm late auntie. I was in Jackson."

"So I heard. Come on in and tell us about it."

Andrew, Fiona and Jeremiah were clustered in the study sipping brandy.

"I guess if everyone's ready we can serve dinner now. Fi- you want to give me a hand?" Petunia said summoning her best friend into the kitchen. "Do you think he's ready for the responsibility Andrew's gonna put on him?"

"I don't really know P. but if there's one thing I do know and that's the fact that we're gonna find out before Tuesday election day. If Darrow can get a victory over Three Winds he's a shoo-in for mayor. I figure he'll hit at the niggras where he knows he'll meet the least resistance and get a nice little militia together with each success and leave Three Winds for last. By then he'll have a large enough army to think there's a good chance of defeating us. And like I said any type of success against us will make him a shoo-in for mayor."

"I can't believe he is still holding his father's death as a reason for attacking us. That had to be close to twenty years ago."

"Some men just grow up bitter and hateful. What he needs is a good woman to love him down real good. That'll take all the fight out of his heathen ass."

Fiona laughed loud and haughtily.

"Girl I don't know why I try to have a serious conversation with you. No matter what the subject it always comes down to sex with you."

"It would be a whole lot betta world if that was first on people's mind."

"You ain't neva lied. I halfway believe you got something there girl."

"I know you Fi- and that's the reason that Jeremiah ain't quite as spry as he used to be."

Fiona grinned widely showing every tooth in her mouth.

"I'm surprised Andrew can even walk. I can remember when the both of us was on him for quite a spell."

Petunia laughed.

"And I'm still trying to wear his monkey ass out," she said the tears running down her face. "Now I wonder though. He gets up and out before the crack of dawn and before I can wrap these pretty little chocolate legs around him. It's almost as if he done got scared of the love. Whatcha think about that Fi-?"

"I think we better get this food on the table before they put us ol' cows out to pasture," she laughed.

Dinner had all the fixings and the trimmings. Caesar commented that it was the best meal he'd had in a month of Sundays to which Petunia replied.

"I guess so living with yo' momma's no cooking ass."

Everyone laughed.

"Caesar I'm sure you're wondering what this is all about," Andrew said looking deep into his nephew's eyes. "The four of us that sit at this table now are the reason we own three hundred thousand acres of the finest farm and grazing land in Mississippi. We used intelligence, cunning, and when necessary armed resistance to make this place our home. And in so doing we made a lot of people angry."

"And then there were a lot of people that were simply angry just because we were niggras," Fiona added.

"And still are…" Petunia added.

"But we did what we had to do to procure the land and protect what is rightfully ours. And often times that meant fighting but never were we the aggressor. We were strong, disciplined, and adamant about holding onto what we had acquired and protecting our women and children and our families."

"I know our history poppa and no disrespect intended but I'm having a hard time understanding why you're telling me this."

"Hush boy," Petunia said raising her voice.

"I think the reason your father is telling you is because he and I have other matters to tend to and it is time we handed the mantle over to the younger men. We have come together as the founders of Three Winds with but one goal in mind and that is to hand to you the keys to every life in our tiny community. What we're asking of you is a huge responsibility but if you ever need help or advice your Uncle Ben will be there to work with you and advise you in any matters pertaining to the security of Three Winds. And of course there are the three of us."

When Andrew finished all eyes were on Caesar who was stunned by this latest edict. Caesar placed his fork down and studied the faces at the table. It was all a bit much. After a few minutes it was Fiona who spoke.

"Son, I know that this is a bit much without prior notice. It also comes at a crucial time for everyone at this table and the community as a whole although most of them are quite unaware of the impending danger but it is a good test for you. We are all aware of Clarence Darrow's intentions. We have all been here before but it is perhaps the best test of your commitment and resolve not only to your family but to the community as well."

The words did little to appease Caesar. What they were asking was for him to accept the responsibility for he and his men but for all of them as well. It just didn't make sense to him especially in light of his recent choice to retire from the military after ten long years. The truth was he had long since come to the moral plateau that questioned his faith in God and the service he had come to question. How long had he trained to kill? And in the end when he came to the conclusion that God had something in store for him other than training to take another man's life he'd relinquished his position. And now this. Again Caesar studied their faces before speaking.

"I feel honored that you've chosen me," he said a tear rolling down his brown cheeks. "But before I commit to anything I must say that I'm curious as to why you chose me with so many other men that are just as capable."

"What we need at this point Caesar and in lieu of what awaits us in the next couple of days is a proven leader and one that has the discipline not to put our community at risk and who has a value for human life," Andrew answered.

"And again I ask you why you chose me?"

"Okay, let's cut through all the bullshit. We all know you have what it takes. After leading sixteen seemingly covert missions…" Petunia said breaking the silence.

"Covert missions my ass," Fiona interjected. "Your auntie's being nice. After leading your unit on sixteen bank robberies and hold ups without having lost or taken a single life we know that you are the best man for the job. And that is hardly to say that any of us here at this table condone your recklessness but it shows us that you are a leader of men and value the lives of all concerned."

"You knew?" Caesar said very much surprised.

Jeremiah grinned broadly.

"I knew we would never get through a meal without one of these women spilling the beans."

"They can't help it. It's in their DNA," Andrew said laughing along with Jeremiah.

"But now since your secret is our secret can we get on with the business at hand," Caesar. "Yours is not an option. You have been groomed for this all of your life and now it's your time to step up. All in favor of Caesar leading the Three Winds Council and militia please say aye."

A chorus of ayes went up.

"It is done then, my son. I am so very proud of you."

"Is there anything you would like to say nephew?" Andrew asked the newly appointed council head.

Caesar was staggered.

"I'm not sure I know what to say at this point," a stern consternation etched his face. "I am not sure at this point whether I have just been blessed or cursed," he said a smile slowly creeping to his face. I just hope I warrant the trust you put in me. And will certainly do my best."

"It probably will seem like a curse at first but with the good you can do it will soon be a blessing." Petunia said before going and hugging her nephew.

The other three congratulated the young man as well.

Chapter 10

"That's right boys we hit 'em tonight."

"They say them dere coons got a small army out there and their well armed. That's what I hear tell."

"I don't care what you hear. Ain't no bunch of wooly headed niggas gonna put nothing over on this here white man. I'll blow half of them to kingdom come and hang the rest. Once we get rid of these niggas life will be better. You'll see. So get ready to kick some ass."

"We headed to Three Winds?"

"Yes, but we don't want to engage them at this time. I think we need a few minor skirmishes to see how cohesive we are as a unit," the tall man with aspirations known as Clarence Darrow said to the small circle around him. "But what I really want to get a bead on is there overall strength. We'll ride in and get a feel for how many troops they got out there and then we can determine what kind of army we can put together. We outnumber them we can whip 'em good."

"If I do recall correctly colonel that's the same thing you told us three years ago when they whipped our asses," Petersen said causing the room to bellow out in laughter.

"And that's why we have to be smarter this time lieutenant."

"I hear you sir but again I have to ask what's going to be any different this time?"

"This time we're committed to having a superior force."

"And how do you plan to put together that many men in only four days before the election?"

"You leave that to me lieutenant."

Meanwhile at Three Winds Andrew and Jeremiah made their rounds. The two were close to inseparable now and being that they were working in earnest their wives could say nothing.

"Have you said anything to Caesar about the best way to defend Three Winds?"

"All his life," Jeremiah replied.

"Recently?"

"I don't think there's a need to speak with him now if I've spoken to him all his life."

"Aren't you even worried in the least bit?"

"Scared to death," Jeremiah laughed," but when we passed the mantle on it was we who entrusted him with our safety. It would not be right in a time of crisis to step in and say we entrust but do not trust you to make good and rational decisions when it comes to our safety and perhaps our lives."

"I guess you are right my friend. I suppose I have been engaged for so long in the day-to-day activities that I cannot just ride off into the sunset."

"Oh I will be there. I will not be in my unusual capacity but if nothing else my aim is still true," Jeremiah grinned.

"Have you at least gone and checked on the overall readiness of the troops?"

"Andrew if I wasn't sure before I am sure now that you are by all means related to Fiona. Never in my life have I seen two people worry as much as you and your sister," Jeremiah laughed. "Come on. Let's check out the site for the new school. The plans are all but complete, the materials in route so let's take one good last look at the site itself. I still think that that hill behind it could end up causing mud slides and flooding."

"A retaining wall will take care of that but aside from that can you really ask for a more aesthetic sight with the clear blue stream running by its side."

Chapter 11

Meanwhile at O'Leary's Pub twelve miles south of Three Winds Clarence
Darrow paid for the drinks of his most trusted lieutenants as he went over the plans for
the night's raids. The pub was crowded as usual. Over to the right of the table where
Darrow addressed his men sat a young farmer who had become a mainstay of O'Learys.
Benjy, Joshua's youngest boy sat sipping a beer his hat pulled down over his brow.

"How many troops can we deploy tonight lieutenant?"

"I'd say at the very least a hundred sir," Lieutenant Petersen said.

"Okay. I want three groups of twenty five to hit the outlying plantations
we mentioned earlier. The fourth and final unit I want under my command. We are
simply gonna reconnoiter and get some vital intel concerning the size and capacity of
Three Winds but some very reliable intel tells me that the niggas out there have grown fat
and have little or no defenses. I know most of you are familiar with Jeremiah—that big
black nigga that used to run security—they tell me he's been sick for some time and had
to retire and one of his sons is running things now. They say he's nothing like his father
so we should have a relatively easy time of it. Any way that's the plan. We ride at

eight." When the men finished the drinks they set out to meet up with their respective units.

Benjy rode hard on the heavily travelled road. His wife had just given birth to their second child and Benjy knew that not only his family but his neighbors and friends were all at risk. It was up to him to get word to Caesar.

Reaching Three Winds he found Caesar relocating the troops. No longer did they line the perimeter. They now stood deep almost a mile within the perimeter. There were no guards at the gates and from an outsider's view it looked as though the settlement was unguarded and that's exactly the way Caesar wanted it to appear.

Andrew and Petunia sat on the front porch, she crocheting and he reading Socrates under a kerosene lantern. A lone firefly dipped in and out of the flickering flame. Closing the book Andrew watched as the firefly despite its fragile makeup darted in and about the flickering flame always somehow managing not to be consumed by the flame. The firefly had come to understand the flame and avoid its being burned. Andrew thought of his own flight and the flight of all those born of color who were always just a hair's breath from the flame when the first shots rang out. He immediately sprang to his feet. Petunia grabbed his arm gently.

"This is no longer our fight Andrew," she said the calm evident in her voice.

"But the boy may need our help," Andrew said the panic obvious in his tone.

"Relax. He'll be fine."

Right about then the handsome black carriage driven by Jeremiah pulled up. Jeremiah helped Fiona out of the carriage.

"Come to see the fireworks? Pull up a chair y'all," Petunia said glad for the company.

"Ever since I can remember we've been together at times such as these so I told Jeremiah we needed to come see you. Although I did half expect to see P. on the front lines calling someone a peckerwood or poor white trash," Fiona said laughing.

"I had to grab Andrew. He heard the first gunshots and headed straight for the gun rack. I've got to be honest I'd much rather be down there than sitting up here with your old asses."

Petunia needed to say no more. Fiona stood quickly and went to her saddlebag and grabbed the Colt.45 and her rifle. Jeremiah followed suit and

Andrew returned quickly with his holster and both his Sharps and Colt revolving rifles. The four followed Jeremiah for a mile or so towards the front gate before Jeremiah pointed out the foxholes where two or three men dressed in all black lay in wait. The four found an empty space in the center of the perimeter where they lay almost as they'd done twenty years before.

They were further back than they'd ever been but then there had to be a reason Andrew surmised. A few minutes later his question was answered as Darrow sent rider after rider in to see just how far they could go and what resistance would be appropriated. When only a shot or two at best was fired Darrow sent all twenty five of his troops while he and Lieutenant Petersen stood back on the bluff and watched though binoculars.

Clarence Darrow was a loud but not a learned man. Overweight he carried the weight of his father's death at the hands of nigga justice along with his air of superiority and entitlement to anyone who would listen. And now here he was at front gate of Three Winds to avenge not only his father's untimely demise but also the South's loss at the hands of niggas and them bleeding heart Northerners.

After the third or fourth charge with little or no resistance Clarence Darrow saw no reason to postpone the siege of Three Winds. He knew all he needed to know. Three Winds was his for the taking. Summoning his forces around him he stepped down from the big gray and white spotted bay.

"We came here tonight to survey the enemy and it's clear that there is little or no resistance. These niggas is so damn arrogant that they done got downright comfortable. They overestimated themselves and if there is one fatal flaw of any army it's never to grow fat and arrogant. These niggas done got fat. It is our job, our birthright to take back what is ours. Long live the South!"

And with that said he unsheathed his sword and led the charge from the dark thicket of trees out over the open grassland into the mouth of the enemy who hadn't fired a shot and lay waiting. As soon as they took to the center of the grassland it was almost as if a sea of black surrounded them, engulfed them and cut them down with a steady and deadly barrage of bullets. Most in attendance had to agree. They never knew what hit them.

It was a sterling and resounding victory for Caesar and all on Thee Winds celebrated the twenty eight year olds first effort as commander-in-chief. But the celebration was short lived when that night there was still no word of Darrow and his men at the rendezvous point at midnight.

An hour later when there was still no word from Darrow his son Byron took charge.

"Guess them niggas is given poppa a little more than he bargained for. Let's see if we can't lend them a hand."

And with a shout that tore them away from their stories of ape and conquest they were up in their saddles off for another skirmish. Arriving at Three Winds they found it quiet.

"From the sounds of things it must be all over," Byron said. "C'mon let's go in and see what we can see?"

"It could be a trap."

"A trap? I think you're giving these niggas far more credit than they deserve. Now load up and let's go."

Minutes later they met the same fate as those that came before them. Only this time Byron who stayed to watch the battle develop and was only there for the spoils managed to sneak away when he saw his men enveloped in a sea of black faces. Making a mad dash to the road he rode hard to Jackson. Arriving there Byron Darrow made his way to the sheriff's office.

It was Friday night and one of the nights the sheriff made it a point to be on duty. Drovers and others always seemed to arrive in town after a long hard week and this is when most of the trouble started. Drunken cowboys who'd been on the trail for weeks were almost always getting into it with the locals and the 'no firearms' edict did little in the way of knife fights and a good ol' round of fisticuffs.

"Sheriff! There's been a massacre. They killed poppa," the young man said the tears cascading down his pale face. Niggas done killed everybody."

"Slow down son. What are you saying," the sheriff said grabbing his holster.

"I'm saying the niggas at Three Winds ambushed us and killed everyone."

"Where did this happen son?"

"At Three Winds."

"On the road?"

"No sheriff. It happened on Three Winds."

The sheriff sat back down and loosened his holster.

"What were you boys doing on Three Winds?"

"Poppa was working on the nigga problem on behalf of the good white folks of Jackson County."

"What you're telling me is that your poppa was trying to make a name for himself by taking on what he considered some poor, defenseless niggas and ran into some well armed niggas that wasn't just gonna roll over and play dead. Now I suppose you want me to go apprehend and try some niggras for doing what any self-respecting white man would do if he felt his life and children's life were in harm's way. I can't go out there and apprehend them niggras for defending themselves."

"You mean poppa's dead and seventy good white men with families and children are dead and you're not going to do anything about it?"

"Son, I was elected to protect the good residents of Jackson. Them niggras at Three Winds don't bother nobody. And they have just as much right as anybody to live in peace. Now if some of the fine residents of Jackson choose to take it upon themselves to leave Jackson and trespass on another man's land to inflict bodily harm then they are responsible for their own safety and well-being. What you're asking me is totally out of my jurisdiction."

"We're talking about niggas sheriff. These niggas killed my poppa. They ain't got no rights."

"Perhaps they ain't got no rights under the law but they feel they have a right under God's law to protect themselves and their families and I will not argue that with them or the likes of you. I'm sorry about your pa but he made his decision and these are the consequences. Accept it boy."

"I'll accept it when they're all dead and I will inform the good residents that the law they elected refused to do anything. I'll raise a posse of my own. We'll take care of them niggas with or without your help."

"You do that and you'll wind up the same way your pappy did."

"We'll just see about that sheriff."

"Listen son. The first thing in the morning I'll ride out and get a firsthand account of what happened. I should be back by noon and I'll let you know what happened. In the meantime I think you should go home and break the news to your momma. I think she's gonna need you close to her side in her hour of need. Now will you do that for me boy? Don't make no sense you going out here and stirring up a town that's half liquored up. All you're gonna do is get some more innocent folks killed. Those niggras at Three Winds are a disciplined, well armed fighting unit. Now can you do that for me boy?"

The young man left the sheriff's office with tears streaming down his face. He was sad and angry. The Lucky Deuce was overflowing, with men screaming and cursing from too much liquor but he knew that the sheriff was right. To gather a posse would be like offering a lamb to the slaughter. No, he unlike his father and his father's father had to have a plan to go up against these here niggas.

The morning came with a pale of death over it. Jeremiah and Andrew worked the burial detail until the wee hours of the morning before retiring.

"Don't you dare feel any type of guilt over tonight, Andrew. Do you hear me? I know how you get after these things and I will not tolerate it. I won't allow it. We have no choice in these matters. We keep to ourselves. It is the hatred in those crackers hearts that led to this. We have no other choice than to defend ourselves. Is it not written in the bible? Blessed be the Lord, my rock, who trains my hands for war, and my fingers for battle. This is written in the bible."

"That makes it no easier P. The death bestowed on those men was not necessary."

"They made it necessary Andrew. Now come to bed my sweet and let me fill you wish nothing but my love."

Two hours later Petunia awoke to the sound of a rider. She nudged Andrew who was dead to the world.

"There's a rider approaching."

"He must be okay if the boys let him through. They're still on duty," Andrew mused.

"Oh, it's the sheriff. Do you want me to see what he wants?"

"You know what he wants P. Tell him I'll be right there."

Moments later Andrew met the sheriff who was already seated on the front porch.

"Morning sheriff."

"Andrew."

"Heard there was little commotion around here last night."

"Nothing out of the ordinary," Andrew said staring at the sheriff. They were not friends, had never been, could not be during these times but there was a mutual respect each had gained for the other over the years.

"A rider came into town last night. That Darrow boy... You know who I'm talkin' about. Said his pappy and seventy some odd of his friends and cronies were massacred right here on Three Winds last night. Now we both know that if those men were on your land then they were trespassing with no good intent. And I believe that every man has a right to protect his own so I won't go any further with that Andrew. But you have to realize what's ahead for you now. If word leaks out that some of our good white citizens were murdered by some niggras I don't have to tell you what type of backlash there will be."

"And you're telling me this why sheriff?"

"You know damn well why I'm telling you this Andrew. That boy wanted me to round up a posse and come out here and have a lynching party. I talked him out of it and sent him home grieving and angry but if that boy gets to talking and stirring up some folks there's going to be hell to pay. I suggest you prepare yourself."

"Thanks for the warning sheriff."

Andrew stood there staring as the sheriff rode off. What had the sheriff told him that he didn't already know? He just hoped that Caesar had the foresight to see what seemed almost inevitable.

Chapter 12

Mandy held the baby tightly as she rode the last few paces.

"Well it's certainly nice to see Caesar hard at work this fine morning. I thought that you'd at least come see your son by now. Buck is wondering if we've done something to offend you. I want to say no you haven't Buck. I have."

"Morning Mandy," Caesar said ignoring her and continuing to chop wood at a steady pace.

"Can we go inside and talk if you don't mind? Here, take your son," she said handing the infant to Caesar before jumping down.

Caesar looked at the baby with loving eyes. Mandy followed the two inside.

"Oh my! The house is lovely Caesar. I know you had help decorating. It's absolutely marvelous."

"Thanks Mandy. Now if you would tell me what's on your mind; I have a lot of work to do."

"What's happened to you Caesar? You didn't use to be so brusque."

"Things have changed Mandy. I've changed. I no longer feel that it's all right hat I'm sleeping with my best friend's wife and have a child by her. It's something I will spend the rest of my life trying to atone for no matter how I feel for you."

"So, there are still feelings for me?"

"If you must know then yes I still have feelings for you. But I can't let my desires come before others especially if it's wrong and sinful. I'd rather cut off my right arm than hurt Buck and I think we've done that already."

"Baby, I hear you and understand. And you're absolutely right but I think you're missing one key element in the whole equation."

"And what's that Mandy?"

"The fact that I've loved you all my life and it's that fact alone that will not allow me to reason and agree with you in all your wisdom," Mandy said smiling broadly.

"Then I don't know what to tell you Mandy."

"Don't want you to tell me anything daddy. Just want you to show me the way you always do," she said grabbing him by the arms and pulling him to her.

"What did the sheriff say?"

"Said he understands but he's certain there will be a devastating backlash that he won't be able to hold off. He bought us some time last night with the Darrow's boy. But he seems to think this will be the worst retaliation yet. They're calling it a massacre."

"Yes, I'd go so far as to say we did a fairly thorough job of it."

"I'm thinking I may gather together some of the fellas around my age and start a little unit of my own just in case."

"You just can't leave it alone can you?"

Andrew smiled. He still had the weight of the world on him and the fact that they were organizing was reason enough for worry but the fact that for the first time in his life he wasn't in charge, in command unnerved him greatly.

"Go talk to Caesar if you're so worried. I'm sure that he can put your mind at rest."

"I think I might just do that. He needs to know the gravity of the situation. I'll let him know what the sheriff had to say."

"There you go. Take an active hand and then you won't feel so helpless."

"See you around noon for lunch P."

"Whatcha want for lunch?"

"You P," Andrew said grinning at the handsome woman before him.

"I'll make sure to keep it hot and ready just the way you like it," Petunia said grinning from ear-to-ear. Oh, how she loved that man.

Andrew rode up to Caesar's house only to be met by screams. Reaching for the long rifle he quickly realized the screams of a woman not in pain but in the midst of a whirlwind of pleasure. He smiled before tearing off a plug of tobacco and finding a seat on the front porch.

A half an hour later the screaming was replaced by an infant's crying and Andrew smiled once again thinking back to when he too was a young man. When the door finally opened he was shocked to see the very same pretty young woman that stood by Buck on the day he was honored for his ten years in the service. Wiping the matted sweat stained hair from her face Mandy smiled at Andrew who simply nodded in acknowledgement.

When she was a safe distance away Caesar turned to his uncle.

"Please don't say anything. I know and I am ashamed uncle. I fear she is my cross to bear."

"I have nothing to say other than the sheriff came to see me and give me fair warning that once the towns people here of what they are referring to as 'the massacre' that took place last night there will be hell to pay. It will be like nothing you've ever seen before so you need to be more than prepared."

"Thank you for the warning uncle. We will be ready."

"Caesar," Andrew said before climbing on the big bay. "The enemy that you are about to face is nothing compared to a woman's wrath who feels she can win your heart and finds out she can't." Andrew said before turning the mount and heading off.

The sound of gunfire suddenly rang out and Caesar grabbed the lone horse tied to the fence post. He was just about to make the rounds and make sure the men were in place when his uncle showed up. Riding fast and hard he soon caught up to his uncle who was also riding fast towards the gunfire. The gunfire was more sporadic as they got closer but still came at a steady staccato.

A quarter of a mile or so up the road they ran into some men coming from the O'Reilly place. A buckboard in tow they rode quickly.

"Caesar they hit our place hard but they were not interested in shelling out any real damage. They were using it simply as a diversion. What they really wanted was Ben. He was leaving his cabin when they hit him."

"Where is he?"

"He's in the buckboard on his way to the hospital."

"How is he?" Andrew said concerned for the man that that was second only to his father in his eyes.

"Ol' Ben's a tough ol' coot. They sent three men in specifically for Ben while they attacked the front gate. They shot him three times. Two are flesh wounds but like I said he's a tough old coot and he held them off with his scatter gun long enough for us to see what they were up to. When we caught up with them Ol' Ben had that ol' scatter gun tucked under his good arm a blazin' away and askin' 'em if that was the best they had. Tickled me. He had 'em pinned down and was talkin' junk to them peckerwoods. But they know they can't beat us head on so now it looks like they're going after those in charge. You be careful Andrew."

"Always Lucious. Thanks for the warning."

Lucious rode off after the buckboard carrying Ben.

"You think what he's saying is true?"

"No doubt in my mind. Lucious served on the council with me as an advisor. He's well versed in the art of war. He knows like I know that if you cut off the head then you kill the body. They know they can't match us in sheer numbers anywhere in Mississippi. I'm just surprised they hadn't thought of that sooner."

"I'm gonna put some people around you uncle."

"I'll be fine."

"Well, then if you don't mind I'd like to have you with me today. If it's all you and the sheriff say it's gonna be I could use your help and advice."

"Would be glad to be of service general," Andrew said as they continued to race towards the sound of the gunfire.

Moments later they were at the frontline. A large body of smoke was growing in the distance.

"Finding his second lieutenant racing up and down the lines shouting commands Caesar grabbed Buck.

"What's all the commotion about?"

"They crossed over into Three Winds about an hour ago. They're trying to outflank us. They hit us hard from the east and west and have been leading charges straight up the middle but so far we're holding pretty well. They've got some fairly good firepower. They've got us pinned down in the middle. Every time we try to raise our heads to return fire they lay down some pretty good cover fire allowing them to advance. I think they've got a Gatling gun."

"Do you have snipers in the field?" Andrew asked.

"The snipers are in place," Caesar said pointing to the trees surrounding the field of battle.

"Then get word to them to train their sights on the Gatling gun and let's use the same strategy on them that they're trying to use on us. I don't know who's leading them but tell them to shoot to maim anyone dressed in a Confederate uniform with an insignia. We get rid of them and this battle should end just that much sooner."

"You heard him Buck. You take the east side and I'll take the west," Caesar yelled before heading west.

Andrew felt better now that he was back in the saddle.

"Stay down men. They'll come again but don't lift your head to fire a shot unless you're life's in danger. Just stay down until we can knock out their big guns."

And come they did but this time there was no return fire. They came behind the sounds of the big gun. Three or four charges did they make firing wildly at an enemy they could not see but there was no retaliatory fire from the front. The men held solidly to their ground waiting for Andrew's command.

And then just as quickly as it had all started it ended with only a shot fired here and there from the trees. When the cloud of dust had dissipated the battleground was empty. It was then and only then that Andrew commanded the troops to proceed forward. Less than a hundred yards away lay a young soldier of no more than twenty three or twenty four draped over the big gun. There were bodies scattered around and a burial team was set up to dispose of them. The men were then assigned new duties and the guard changed to keep them fresh. When all was seemingly calm Andrew found Caesar and conferred with him on the current state of affairs.

"They probably won't return 'til tonight but I think it's time to identify the ring leaders and then I want your unit to split into teams and find these ringleaders in their homes and make short work of them. Then in the middle of the night I want these men who lead armies against woman and children to be hung in the town square to show all of

Jackson what happens when you disturb the peace and tranquility of Three Winds. It's time we ended this madness once and for all."

"Are you sure that's what you want to do uncle? I know that they shot Ol' Ben and you're angry but do you think that attacking them in their homes in front of their wives and children and then putting them on public display for all the town to see is the right thing to do? That just portrays us as the same monster that we're fighting against. Violence may beget violence but we will only incur evil if we act in the same evil and malicious way."

Andrew took a step back and looked at the young man before him knowing that he was right but so strong was his anger and his passion that he could no longer speak. How long had he fought? As long as he could remember he had had to succumb to this evil curse led by the devil himself and he was tired. How hard had it been to be both a leader of men and a follower of Christ when a southern man's bible did not foster the same beliefs that a niggras did.

"Carry on young man. Carry on with the patience and righteousness that this old man no longer has."

Chapter 13

The crowd milling outside the sheriff's door was in a foul mood having been bested by them rogue niggas three times in as many days.

"Sheriff you have got to do something. As if it weren't bad enough that these niggas ain't got no objection to murderin' good white men they done built an army out there and are daring us to set foot on land that was originally the colonel's land. If the colonel could see what was going on he'd roll over in his grave. Lord that man would rise from the grave if he knew niggas was running Three Winds."

"What I think you boys are failing to understand is that the colonel is dead and his wife the sole proprietor after his death willed the land to her niggras and they are now the sole proprietors of Three Winds and no matter how much better you think you are than those niggas at Three Winds they are the lawful owners of that piece of property and if you go out there and onto their land then you are trespassing. I think your best bet would be to go on about your business before y'all get yourselves killed. Now that's my advice to y'all. I'm gonna tell you and I know the niggra out there that's runnin' things and he ain't nothing to be messed with."

"Are you tellin' us that you's afraid of a bunch of niggas sheriff?"

"T'ain't afraid of no one 'cept for the Lord God Almighty but I knows when I'm in over my head and if I was you I wouldn't let Byron Darrow lead me into no situation trying to avenge his pappy and grand pappy. Look at where they is? And if you don't wanna join them I suggests you take your asses home."

"Alright sheriff. I never thought no Fernhill man would ever be scair't of no niggas. Or is it that you just done gone and turned nigga lover?"

Sheriff Fernhill who stood a good six inches taller and weighed a good forty or fifty pounds more than the man swung once sending the man sprawling into the crowded street.

There was no more talk of the sheriff being a nigga lover but that hardly ended the conversation. It was Byron Darrow who spoke now.

"Sheriff I don't give a fuck if you're with us or you're not I just want you to know that I'm the one that's gonna lead the charge this time. I plan on carrying on my father's work and that includes running for mayor.

At this very moment I'm enlisting good white southern gentleman from all across the state that believe that niggas need to stay in their place and don't have no place alongside of the likes of me and my brothers here. Within a week or so we'll have enough good southern white men in Jackson to get rid of them niggas once and for all.

I don't know what side you'll be on sheriff but you may want to get your mind right and get behind us or you're gonna look really bad when elections come around again and the good citizen of Jackson ask why there was all of this chaos under your watch."

Close to three hundred white men from in and around Jackson milled around with bottles, firing into the air and screaming obscenities while others stood around content to listen to the lies and work up the courage to join their clansmen.

That was Saturday afternoon. By the evening those drunk enough to mount a charge made their way out to Three Winds where they were sprayed and peppered with sniper fire. Returning to Jackson later that evening, their egos destroyed they poured more and told lies of thousands of niggas all armed and waiting to ambush them along the road to town. Now those who had no part or inkling to get involved ran home in fear and loaded their guns.

"I'm not sure what you told Caesar isn't a bad idea after all. This is the third time they've hit us this weekend and it's only Saturday," Petunia said.

"It's one thing to be on the defensive but it's another thing to be passive and invite this type of treatment. Lucious tells me that they're taking pot shots from high up on the bluff of the children bathing," Jeremiah said. "I just left him."

"Oh, hell no," Fiona shouted. "What they need is a wakeup call. They need to know that these niggras here ain't just gonna lie down to they kind of shit. What we need to do is to take the fight to them. We need to set up camp right down on Main Street and dare them to walk the streets in their own town without fear of retribution. See how they like that shit then. But the first thing we need to do is get that Byron Darrow. He's the ringleader and instigator of all this shit. If y'all wit' me let me see a show of hands."

All hands went up in unison and it was now only a matter of devising a plan that hit hard and without provocation that would send a sign that said there would be zero tolerance for any more attacks on Three Winds or its inhabitants.

Andrew insisted on making their grievances known prior to attacking that way if there did exist any good, lawful folks in Jackson they could make arrangements and stay clear of the agitators and troublemakers.

"Send a messenger to the sheriff and tell him that I want a one-on-one meeting with Mr. Darrow. I want no one there but the mayor and Mr. Darrow. Should he be accompanied by anyone other than the mayor I will look at it as an act of aggression and will shoot to kill. Make that understood."

Two hours later the messenger returned.

"The streets are full of men hollerin' and cussin about how many niggas are gonna die before the night is over."

"Did you get my message to the sheriff?"

"Yes sir Mr. Andrew. The sheriff said he and Mr. Darrow will meet you by the North Fork in an hour."

"Thank you son," Andrew said to the young lad of ten or eleven.

"Anyone heard from Joshua or his boys?"

"They're saying almost the same thing as the boy just did. They say the streets are crowded with angry white folks and there are more riding in all the time."

"That's okay. It's just an excuse for them to get all likkered up and form a lynch mob. The more they drink the better. It's a hell of a lot easier to fight a drunken mob than a disciplined well-oiled fighting unit."

"From what Joshua tells me Darrow sent out a letter to the state legislature to mandate the usage of a volunteer militia at the hint of a niggra uprising in the making. At this very moment Darrow is getting ready to send out couriers to solicit men to join his volunteer army. Says he should have at least a thousand men by the end of the week."

"Make that your first priority and put a couple of men on each courier. Don't let them deliver that message," Petunia said upon her arrival. "And we need someone to pull Darrow's coat. He may need some persuasion. All he's doing is trying to get into office and we're to be his example of how we niggras need to return to slavery or some fashion of it. What they fear most is us being on equal terms with them. For some reason they really and truly believe they are superior to us."

"Why is that auntie?"

"I don't know Caesar but I'm here today to let them know that I am not in agreement with their premise. What I want you to do Caesar is to take half your unit and return with Darrow and take the other half and put them on those couriers. Andrew I want you to check on Ben. Jeremiah I want you to stay with the troops and tell the snipers to look sharp and keep a keen eye out. As far as you Ms. Fiona… if you don't

mind may I have the honor of having you by my side as I go inspect the troops and offer

some words of moral support."

"You certainly may Ms. P. just let me get my gun."

The sudden arrival of Petunia brought with her a concise and determined plan and

none of the others were in any way taken aback by Petunia's incursion. All of them were

capable of leading after having been in a multitude of skirmishes and battles over the

years.

Taking their leave Caesar found his way to Buck and put him on the couriers with

Joshua's boys leading the way so as to diminish resistance should they run into any of the

town's folks. He would take Darrow himself. From what Benjy told him Darrow spent

much of the early evening at The Lucky Deuce but headed for the O'Leary's to see if he

couldn't recruit some more men with the intentions of attacking again tonight.

Caesar reasoned that although Darrow knew his men didn't stand a chance the

fatalities will do just as well with his election bid. He was running on 'the nigga

problem' and every death by the hands of niggas would only support his cause. After all

they were the problem. Once they were eliminated good white folks would return to the prosperity they knew and had come accustomed with niggras doing the heavily lifting and the burden of the work. According to the Darrows that was the key.

A quarter of a mile from O'Leary's Caesar posted four men on each side of the road. According to Benjy's account there were two other men travelling with him. Short and stocky with a wide girth Byron Darrow posed no real physical threat. And it was not long before the three men were in the custody of Caesar's elite unit.

Cutting through the woods on the way back Caesar listened to the man's idle chatter.

"You niggas done lost your mind. You think you can go from slave to master just like that? I don't know what you missed boy but if you heathens could read you'd see that it says specifically that you were put here to be our servants. It says so if you read Ephesians 6:5. It says and I quote:

> Slaves, obey your earthly masters with respect and fear, and with sincerity of heart, just as you would obey Christ."

Caesar stared at the short, stocky man and smiled.

"I am afraid if you had read further my good man you would have noticed the next passage from Ephesians which states:

> "And masters, treat your slaves in the same way. Do not threaten them, since you know that he who is both their Master and yours is in heaven, and there is no favoritism with him."

The short, stocky white man was shocked by Caesar's reply.

"Looks like we got a learned, uppity, nigga in our presence boys," Darrow laughed.

"Yes and the funny thing about it is this learned, uppity nigga has the fate of you and your two friends in the palm of his hand.

And right now I'd say you're mighty lucky Mr. Darrow. If the ladies on the council have anything to do with sentencing you for your crimes I have a strong feeling that you'll be reunited with your pappy and grand pappy before this night is over."

And for the first time since he'd been abducted did the man begin to listen to the tall, firmly built niggra and acknowledge his fate.

A half an hour later they approached Three Winds with Darrow and his men in tow. A few minutes later Buck rode in with six of the couriers escorted by his unit.

"Two of them got away but I don't think they're going to cause us too many problems. One's gut shot and I'm pretty sure I winged the other one. Were you able to get Darrow?"

"The men are taking him to the council circle as we speak."

"Any word on Ben?"

"From what they tell me he's already been released and is already on his way to join the military tribunal at the circle. Uncle Andrew has sent word to join us there as soon as we get back."

"Guess we should head that way then," Buck said.

The days were full of excitement for everyone and it was at these times when one could see the camaraderie of all those at Three Winds. Women and children pitched in to bring the soldiers food and drink on the front lines while young lovers came to visit there men and offer words of encouragement. Those that had no families went to the hospital to help with the wounded and sick. Everyone was involved for the common good.

Jeremiah kept the troop's intact while deep in the woods stood thirty or more men of African descent. These ex-slaves adorned in all black with black masks to cover their faces posed quite a threatening presence with their machetes.

"In light of the past three days where no resident of Three Winds has stepped foot off the place and has issued no aggression to anyone we still find ourselves on the defensive. Mr. Darrow has made charges on three separate occasions with the intent of murdering the innocent folk of our community simply because of our skin color.

They have transgressed and trespassed with the sole intent of murdering innocent men, women and children as if they were sheep for slaughter.

Today they went so far as to attack the O'Reilly Place shooting our patriarch, brother and friend Ben. And so for these crimes against humanity I will let our oldest and most revered council member and victim of these violent transgressions pass sentence against these men and the leaders of this vigilante," Petunia said.

Andrew helped Caesar carry Ben to the chair facing the men now kneeling on the ground before him.

Ben stared at the three white men for some time before speaking.

"I have always believed in the Good Book. I have studied the words of my Lord Jesus Christ hoping to gain both guidance and understanding. He is a good and just God who teaches us to turn the other cheek when confronted with violence and evil. And those that are old enough to recollect know that I have always tried to adhere to his teachings. I am an old man with only a few moons left. I have weathered the storm of the white man's discontent for what seems like forever. I have as impossible as it seems grown accustomed to it so I would deem it only the Christian thing to do to release these men to their conscious and their God."

Everyone in attendance gasped.

"To let them go would only give them a short reprieve and with all the malice in their hearts they would be back with the same wicked intentions. Ben continued.

"If I were a strong man, a good Christian that is what I would do. I'd give them a pass but I regrettably still have a ways to go in that area and so I sentence you that do Mr. Darrow's work to hang by the neck until death and for you Mr. Darrow I sentence you to be tortured and then hung and burned so no other Darrow will ever spring from your loins and be able to spew the hate and venom that you are so full of. I, therefore, decree death to these men," Ben said summoning Andrew.

In his ninety some odd years Ben had seen too much unnecessary death in his lifetime. At ninety he had yet to find a good meaning for men killing other men.

No sooner than Ben decreed death than Fiona was up and moving toward Darrow. Grabbing the machete she was on him before anyone knew it.

"Why do you need ears peckerwood? God gave them to you and yet you refuse to listen. You are not better than me white man and never will be. All you had to do was accept that and God's glory and live your life. But no you choose to impose your will, your hatred on me and my people who have never done anything to you. You do not hear God talking to you and so I ask you again why do you need ears when you do not listen?" Fiona said grabbing the man by the ear and lopping it off with one fell swoop of the machete.

Fiona remembered being a young girl—she couldn't have been more than eleven or twelve—when those white men—there were four of them that night that raped her down by the creek. She'd never been able to understand it but it had made an indelible mark that said she would never trust because they were after all the devil's incarnate on earth. She felt no mercy let alone remorse as she sliced and sliced at the man's skin. Byron Darrow screamed every time Fiona would rise from the old, oak, tree hollow and approached.

"My God! I am so sorry. Please dear God! I repent my Lord. I will change my ways. I pray fo' God to show some mercy. Lord please don't let this nigga bitch cut me no more!"

At which time Fiona would run the point of the machete from the tip of his shoulder cutting the muscle so his arm just dangled now to the top of his thigh letting the blood ooze out. She'd become rather skilled at surgical technique from her time practicing medicine in the hospital. Careful not to cut any arteries and have the short, stocky man bleed out Fiona sliced his flesh at odd angles and watched him shriek in pain as the blade sliced slivers from his flesh.

"Please tell me why white folks can't just acknowledge that we different and let it go at that. Do we come to y'alls house and try to kill yo' families? Hell no. Black folks ain't built like that. We pretty much keeps to ourselves. But not you. Why you filled with so much hate white man? Did I do something to you white man? No, I couldn't of. You see I ain't never seen or met you before. Has you ever met me before? No you ain't never met me befo' so what is it that makes you hate me so white man? Oh never mind white man. I don't believes you know yo'self."

Caesar watched in disbelief. It was no different than watching a hog butchered other than that a hog being butchered was swift and deadly so as not to cause the animal any pain. No, that was not like this at all but the torturing of the man though it bothered

him somewhat what bothered him more was seeing his own mother who had always been

so gentle with he and his siblings filled with an ugly, hatred that bordered on insane

cruelty and he wondered what it was that made her so angry. Then as he listened to her

words and combined them with Ben's he understood how cruel and inhumane slavery

must have been.

The three days following the hangings Three Winds was quiet. All seemed to be

returning to normal when the sheriff rode up.

"How's everything Andrew?"

"Fair to middlin'. I'm blessed. Every day I'm above ground I'm blessed."

"Ain't that he truth. I think we've both got more good days behind us than in

front of us."

"This aging thing ain't particularly a blessing," Andrew laughed, "I have aches

and pains in places I didn't even know I had."

Both men laughed.

"I was just on my way out back to the garden. I think the deer are eating up my tomatoes and pole beans. Petunia wants me to put a fence around it but I don't want to do anything. As far as I'm concerned the deer can have it."

The sheriff laughed.

"I miss something sheriff?"

"Well when you said garden I thought I'd go for a walk and get my morning exercise and a good laugh while you tell me some more tall tales about how men keep heading this way and disappearing into thin air. I expected to see a real garden. What you got here? About four tomato plants and five corn stalks?"

"You gotta remember back sheriff. After all the hours I spent in the fields I ain't particularly fond of no fields or no gardens."

Both men laughed heartily.

"So what brings you out here today sheriff?"

"Do you consider us friends Andrew?"

Andrew who was usually on his toes had to stop and take pause.

"I'm not sure of how to take that sheriff. My wife tells me that you are a good man but I don't know. And I'll tell you why I don't know."

"This I'm sure should be good. Let's sit my knee is acting up again."

The two men made their way over to the shade of a weeping willow.

"You were saying?"

"I was saying that I think you're a good and fair white man as far as white men go."

"I don't believe I asked you if you thought I was fair or good. I believe my question to you was are we friends?"

"I would say this to you and to any white man that asked me something like that although you are the first and in all likelihood probably the last that would ask me that. It is hard to trust any white man in lieu of what they have put me through. So, no I cannot say that I have any white friends nor do I have a hankering for any. I simply do not trust white folk."

"That is sad to hear Andrew because I believe you to be one of my friends. I think before one becomes friends he must first have respect for that person. I have the utmost most respect for you Andrew. I don't quite understand why Missy Anne willed you the land," he said rolling his eyes to the sky as if he had an inkling, "but I see how hard you have worked and made it a prosperous community despite the hardest of economic times. I only wish I could convince some of the townspeople to follow your lead instead of following poor white trash like Darrow and blaming anybody but themselves for the situation they find themselves in."

"It's always easier to find a scapegoat."

"That it is and speaking of Mr. Darrow..."

"Who was speaking of Mr. Darrow? I sure as hell wasn't. I'm inclined to let sleeping dogs lie."

"I guess that means you haven't seen him?"

"Can't say that I have but the day is still young."

"Last thing I heard was that he was taking up his dead father's work and running for mayor and then he just vanished."

"From what I hear he didn't have much of a platform to run on. What was it? The nigga problem... Think his pappy and grandpappy ran on the same platform. Didn't fare no better for them."

The sheriff laughed.

"That's funny you should say that. You know the old man, the grandfather was a Confederate officer and was a mean old cracker but his son wasn't much of a thinker and tried to follow on his daddy's coattails but you know I told both Clarence and his son Benjy that they may not want to mess with Three Springs but no they was hard-headed and thought they was still gonna get rich offa the backs of niggras. And now they've seem to have just disappeared. It's funny how things turn out isn't it?"

"It certainly is."

"I ain't never said nothing 'bout their disappearances though have I? I have never investigated their disappearance have I?"

"No. Not that I know of sheriff."

"And the reason I have never said anything is because I consider you a friend Andrew and because I believe my friend has a right to defend his land and his people. Any man that interferes with that is subject to whatever befalls him."

"And you're telling me this why?"

"Because I want us to be friends."

"If it means so much to you then I will say I am your friend."

"Then as my friend I must tell you that before that last Darrow died or disappeared he was trying to recruit an army. He sent couriers out. Now that I think about it none of them returned and brought any men with them."

"Perhaps they didn't make it," Andrew said smiling and looking at the ground.

"Is there something that you know that you're not telling me?"

"Isn't there always?"

"But that's not how friendships are made. I tell you things that will help aid you and your people and every now and then you're supposed to share some piece of information that helps me to do my job."

"Oh, I see sheriff. You just asked me if I was your friend. You never explained the rules."

"Well yes Andrew. As friends we share information."

"Oh, well in that case my wife—you know my wife—well she fashioned the whole Darrow plan. You see she kidnapped him, then tortured, hung and burned him to death."

"Your wife had this done?"

"Yes. You know my wife Petunia?"

"Yes I know Ms. Petunia," he said knocking the ashes from his pipe and looking out of the corner of his eye at Andrew. He had never been able to figure Andrew out and now that they were friends hardly made it any easier.

"Well, Andrew I do not know if I should believe you or not but because I consider you my friend I will share this bit of information with you. Before Mr. Darrow was taken from us he was doing his best to recruit a militia to take on you and your folks. Called himself spearheading the drive to eliminate niggras from Jackson. As I told you he sent out couriers but he also wrote letters to the governor and others in the government. You know his family was crucial to the governor gaining office.

In any case, the governor is supposedly sending investigators to look into the disappearance of those seventy men. His threat to me was that all this would happen under my watch. And it looks like it will. I have to lend my full cooperation which means I will probably be bringing troops and investigators onto Three Winds in search of those men.

I am sorry to have to infringe on you and your people's privacy but it shouldn't take them more than two or three days to snoop around. You and I both know they won't find anything on Three Winds or anywhere else so just bear with us during this whole charade Andrew."

The sheriff then stood and made his way back around to the front of the house.

"And Lord knows try to have some humility Andrew. Whether they be northerners or southerners I don't suppose they're going to be too many white folks that are going to be thrlled by your homes and your prosperity when the nation is still struggling to recover and get back on its feet from the war."

"I will do my best to 'suh. I believes I can still shuffle some suh."

"That is not what I meant."

"Isn't it? I doubt that any man would tell you to be humble or how to act in front of another man."

"Andrew I have no problem with you being a man but then they have always talked about me being different but most men are adamant about the way niggras are supposed to behave and anything out of the norm can come with hardship. I'm just telling you that you can catch more bees with honey."

"I have no interest in bees. I think they are more interested in me than I in them. And for their sake I just hope that they act with respect when they are on Three Winds."

"Don't know what else I can say Andrew. I tried," the sheriff said mounting his horse.

"Thank you my friend," Andrew said as the sheriff rode off. The sheriff never heard.

Chapter 14

Mandy sat on the front porch in the wooden rocking chair she'd always loved so much. Caesar had fashioned it for her when she turned sixteen and said he would always keep it for her. Whenever she would go to see him it would be there. Back when they were kids if she told him she was coming he'd have Fiona bake a little something and always have it waiting in her favorite chair out front.

They'd planned to be married back then but something or other was always delaying their plans until Caesar or she had both lost hope that they would ever be married.

In her frustration she'd threatened him. If he didn't take time out to marry her she'd marry Buck who liked her anyway. When Caesar hadn't even bothered to answer she did exactly that.

A year into the marriage she came to the sudden realization that she didn't, couldn't and wouldn't ever love Buck. She was still in love with Caesar. As far as

Caesar was concerned she was still his and he continued to treat her the same way as he had before she was married sleeping with her every chance he could. Well, that was up until he'd fallen in love with Celeste.

Now that chair that held the cakes and preserves was just a chair to Caesar who by now maintained a nice little stable of single fillies who would have given a right arm to be with him. Caesar hardly saw them either. And the home he'd built expecting it to be Celeste's home remained just a house.

Mandy never did understand. She knew how he made her feel when they laid down in each other's arms. She could only surmise that despite his quiet nature she made him feel the same way too. So, then why was it so hard to take the next step?

Buck used to always tell her that he would never hold her should she want to leave. No, it was Caesar who was still bashful when it came to claiming her and making her his wife.

Mandy was quickly awakened from her dreams. By now she was used to dreaming wide awake especially when it came to Caesar and matters of the heart.

"Mandy, what have I told you about just showing up?"

"Caesar please. I'm not in the mood for your bullshit. Take me in the house and make good love to me. Don't say a word. Do you hear! Just bed me down real good.

Caesar grabbed the woman's hand as if he were grabbing a bale of hay and pulled her into the house and then upstairs to the bedroom. Locking the door he dropped his pants revealing an erection that would have made most women wince. But Mandy wasn't most women. Seeing him she looked deeply into his eyes before letting her dress fall. He lifted her and placed her gently on his granite hard shaft.

Hearing riders coming, Caesar lay Mandy down on the bed and made his way to the window.

"Where's your horse?"

"I walked," she said gathering her petticoats around her.

"Stay put," he said closing the bedroom door behind him.

Moments later he returned.

"Who was it?"

"Just a messenger."

"Then come back to bed lover," she said beckoning him once more.

Caesar stared at the young woman lying seductively across his bed.

"Mandy sweetheart, I'm sorry I just can't do this anymore. It's wrong. It's not who I am anymore. It's not where I want to be."

"I don't know exactly what that means but the feeling I get is that you feel you've outgrown me. I think you've finally come to believe all the talk. You think you're better than me. After all you are a member of Three Winds royalty and I am no more than a slave girl sold up river for you to bed down whenever it pleases you."

"I never said that and you and I both know that I don't think like that."

"You know that I love you. I've always loved you. It's just that I don't know that I'm in love with you anymore Mandy and I really hate the situation it puts me in. I don't know that I can stop these visits but together we have got to try."

"You used to be in love with me. What made it change? Is it Celeste?"

"I haven't seen Celeste in over a year Mandy. That's ludicrous. Why is it so hard for you to accept the fact that people simply mature and grow apart? The things that we used to talk about just don't seem to matter as much anymore in light of other things."

"So, you've matured and grown up and left me behind. Is it because I know nothing of the world outside of Three Winds? Is it because I can't read or write? Is it because I am not worldly like you and your little schoolteacher friend?"

"I've already told you that I have not seen or talked to Celeste."

"When your son was born I did not see or talk to you for six months but that did not mean that my heart did not cry out in agony to be with the man I loved. From a woman's eyes that is exactly what I see. You built this house for Celeste and you to grow old in but it's obvious to everyone but you that she too has fallen out of love leaving you no different than me despite your travels and worldliness. Am I right Caesar?"

She had never seen him cry. Was she about to now? Caesar aware of Mandy's stare quickly regained his composure.

"You're right Mandy? It's going on two years and I must admit I'm as much in love with her as I've ever been and I guess until I have closure where she's concerned I will never be able to have a relationship with anyone?"

"I fear we have both been left to hang out to dry. But the solution to your little problem may aid us both."

"I don't think I fully understand. But Lord knows if you have a solution Mandy please let me know. It's been close to a year now and I have never been in such misery in all my life."

"Don't you worry your pretty little head about it. Give me time and let Ms. Mandy work it out for you but for now what Ms. Mandy needs is for you to work this out for me," she said leaning back on the bed.

The two made love until both were tired and spent. When they awoke in each other's arms it was early evening.

"I could stay right here in your arms 'til tomorrow if you'd just ask," Mandy said gazing into Caesar's big brown eyes. "But I already know the answer to that so let me get up and head home."

"Take my horse and drop it off with my father. It's a short walk from there."

"Such a gentleman and trust me I will remedy your problem for you, for us."

Puzzled Caesar was too tired to question the petite little mulatto woman climbing out of his bed. Mandy was as beautiful as any woman on the place and in all of Jackson County for that matter and a lioness in bed but no matter how beautiful she could not be his if he did not love her. And this she couldn't understand.

The days and nights came and the summer was slowing losing its battle to fall. The soldiers hadn't shown and all seemed to be returning to normal but Andrew and Petunia had their reservations.

"It's been too quiet P," Andrew said over their morning coffee as P. commented on the chill in the morning air.

"Oh, things are sure to pick up right abruptly when Buck finds out his wife is sleeping with Caesar. Someone's bound to die in that little love triangle."

"So, you know about that?"

"I think the only person that doesn't know about it is Buck."

"You know I went by the new house when I was thinking about putting him in charge of the troops and she was there then with the baby. I warned him then."

"Now it makes me wonder who the baby's father really is."

"I think it best if we just leave it alone and let it just work itself out."

"I had no plan on going anywhere near that. That's nothing but trouble if you ask me. But it wouldn't hurt o speak to your son Andrew."

"I couldn't agree more but I was talking about the investigation. It's funny that we haven't heard or seen anyone and it's been close to a month since I talked to the sheriff. Just seems mighty strange."

"Why don't you ride in and ask him if it's on your mind."

"Nahh… I think what I'm gonna do is send all five of Joshua's boys into town and see what they can pick up."

"You can do that tomorrow."

"Remind me."

The morning came in just as the night had gone out somber and cold and with the morning came the sound of small footsteps. Caesar reached over and eased the forty-five from the nightstand and placed it on his thigh under the covers. Cocking the hammer as the door slowly opened Caesar relaxed seeing Mandy.

"You might as well have spent the night," he said wiping the sleep from his eyes, "if I had known you'd be back at the crack of dawn."

He slid the gun from under the covers and placed it back on the night stand.

"Oh my! Two guns today," she said disrobing and sliding under the covers. "I like that one okay but I really like this one so much better," she said mounting him and sliding his member into her.

"C'mon daddy! Make me see the moon and the sky like you did last night."

On the edge of releasing all the demons within he heard riders fast approaching.

"Wait here."

Caesar dressed quickly throwing an overnight shirt on to cover his tall, broad frame he raced to the front door only to find Buck standing there ready to enter.

"What's the good word my friend?"

"Nothing C. Just going out on our morning patrol up by Jackson to do a little reconnoitering is all. Thought you might want to ride up with us."

"Not this morning Buck. I'm in the midst of something presently," he said smiling sheepishly. Knowing exactly what his friend was alluding to Buck mounted his horse and turned to his men.

"Don't think Caesar wants to go see what's cooking up around Jackson. I think he's doing a little stir frying of his own." The men laughed. "You need to do what I did C. It's time for you to settle down and get a wife. There comes time when all that fornicating and sinnin' has to come to an end," he said before riding off to a chorus of laughter. Caesar returned to his bedroom visibly shaken.

"Who was that?"

"That was your husband," Caesar sighed.

"Don't worry about him baby," Mandy said sliding down under the covers. "I'll take care of your problem as well as my own. I promise you that. Just give me a little time daddy."

Caesar sat on the edge of the bed and closed his eyes. Buck's passing through only sealed his thoughts. His affair with Mandy had to end. He'd been involved with her

for as long as he could remember but it was different now. She'd made her choice and she needed to honor her commitment and if she chose not to then it couldn't be with him.

He loved Mandy. He always had but she'd chosen to marry his best friend as a way of spiting him for not committing. He had to admit it stung at first but he'd never spoken upon it to her or anyone else.

At first he withdrew from life but in the course of time she found her way back to the only man she'd ever loved and after a couple of years of communal visits he'd become careless. The affair was now obvious to more than a few and he was only too surprised Buck hadn't found out about it yet. But today had been far too close a call and it had to stop.

Mandy had no intentions of putting an end to the relationship and on several occasions it almost seemed that she was doing her best to be found out. He, on the other hand had too much to lose. He would almost certainly lose his oldest and dearest friend along with the respect of his command. And then there was the community where he was looked upon as a leader. Mandy was intent on destroying all that and more. No, something had to be done and quickly.

Mandy had the same thoughts. There were too many obstacles in the way of her and her man. Somehow Buck and Celeste needed to leave Three Winds.

"Get up Mandy. I want you o go home and stay there. I don't want to see you again 'til you hear from me. At this rate you're going to get one of us killed. Do you hear me? Just give me some time to work this out," Caesar said looking through the woman now standing before him.

"I'll be waiting to hear from you. In the meantime I'll be doing the same. There just has to be a solution baby. And please be quick about it sugar. You know one day without you in my life is too long," she said kissing him on his forehead before leaving.

Caesar sat back contemplating his next move. If he didn't handle the Mandy situation there would definitely be hell to pay.

In the following weeks Caesar considered his uncle's words closely. The life of one can be disposed of in lieu of the good of the entire community. In growing up he'd heard tales of people having to be killed that threatened the welfare of Three Winds. Could he add Mandy to the list? In the coming weeks he gave the matter considerable thought. When he hadn't heard from her he left the idea alone. He had other more important matters to tend to. The ranch was thriving and once every couple of months he had Benjy go into Jackson with a string of horses to do his bidding. The horse trade was profitable and Caesar boasted having the finest stock of thoroughbreds in Jackson County.

It was on one such visit into Jackson that Benjy was in the company of a girl he was particularly sweet on when he inquired as to where her father was as he was always in the market for some prime horse flesh.

"Oh, poppa's in town with the sheriff and the major," the girl said.

"The major?" Benjy asked.

"Yes, you know the army major who was brought in to quell the niggra problem out there at Three Winds. They say those niggras massacred close to a hundred white men. They're getting ready for a major assault on them niggras in a day or two. You haven't heard? It's all the talk. They say the major's got more than a thousand troops waiting on the outskirts of town and is just waiting for the rest to arrive before striking a blow on behalf of all the good white folk of Jackson. Poppa says he hopes he wipes out all those shiftless, lazy niggras."

Shocked Benjy sat and listened as the young girl went on and on about the soldiers before taking his leave.

"I thought you were going to wait for poppa. He should be back shortly."

"No. I have a few more stops to make. Tell him I stopped by and I'll try to stop back by tomorrow."

"I look forward to seeing you then Benjy."

What had it been? A month since Darrow had attacked them. Benjy rode hard and fast. All he'd known growing up was these niggras. To him they'd always been family. He'd grown up with Caesar and Caesar was like one of his own brothers. Now it was his duty to let them know what lay ahead in the coming days but Lord was he tired and he wasn't even a niggra.

Lord knows what those people had to go through. At least he could walk the streets without having to move or step aside when some poor white trash came along. He could frequent the saloons and Delmonico's without being harassed. Now this... He was tired of being the bearer of bad news. And this was the worst possible news.

"Mr. Andrew. Mr. Andrew," Benjy said pulling up at the livery stables. "I just came from Jackson. They have troops—over a thousand of them and they plan to attack Three Winds in the next day or so. The only reason they haven't attacked us already is because they're waiting for more troops."

Andrew was used to news of this sort and took it all in stride.

"Whoa, whoa, whoa! Slow down boy," he said grabbing the prancing horse's reins. "Calm down and tell me what this is all about."

Benjy recounted the story the girl had told him as Andrew pulled out his pipe and filled it with tobacco. When he finished he was surprised to see the older man's expression had not changed.

"Mr. Andrew did you hear me? U.S. troops are getting ready to attack us."

"Calm down Benjy. Everything will be fine. What I need for you to do now is to get your father, Caesar, Jeremiah, Fiona and send someone dependable over to the O'Reilly's for Ben and see if he's fit to ride. Can you do that for me boy?"

"Yes sir."

"And Benjy…"

"Sir?"

"Don't speak a word of what you heard to anyone. We don't need anyone panicking."

"Yes sir."

Andrew sat down on the hollow tree stump by the livery stables. How often had he come here to think over the years? He was oh so tired. Why couldn't white folks just leave them to live in peace? In all his life niggras had never been the aggressor. Never and yet they were constantly fighting a never ending battle.

"Oh Lord, when Andrew finds this tree stump that can only mean one thing and that's that he's carrying the weight of the world on his shoulders. What's wrong now my love?"

He smiled at the one constant in his life.

"Just got news from Joshua's youngest. From what he tells me there are over a thousand troops on the other side of Jackson and they're waiting for more."

"Oh my God! Did he say if they were federal or just local militia?"

"He didn't say. It hardly matters though. He says their intention is to attack us without provocation based on rumors that we massacred over a hundred good white folks."

"And based on rumors they're..." Petunia started.

"Yes," Andrew said interrupting his wife.

"How can they come on our land? That's trespassing. Don't we even have a say?"

"You know we have no rights and no say so all we can do at this point is to defend ourselves."

"But this ain't Darrow Andrew. This could be the federal government."

"Yes, and if it is they're going on the word of some bigoted crackers. But no matter who it is we've got to defend ourselves and our land. Listen I've sent for Jeremiah and Fiona and the rest. They should be here by and by. Talk to them and set up a good defense. Call up the reserves. I want every man, woman, boy and girl that can hold a rifle out there. Have them interspersed with the troops.

They won't expect us to be ready so I want them hit them on the road before they get to Three Winds. That should get rid of a large part of his forces if we can ambush them and catch them in the crossfire. Then I want them to fall back and hit them again about a quarter mile from there. This time I want just the snipers and tell them to aim for the officers. I want them stunned and in total disarray by the time they put foot on Three Winds. And the minute they cross onto Three Winds I want every gun trained on them. I want them to know that they're in a war. I'm going in to Jackson and see what I can find out from the sheriff."

"No, Andrew. It's far too dangerous for any niggra to be seen in Jackson right through here if what you're telling me is true."

Andrew ignored his wife and stood ready to mount the stallion when Petunia fired a shot.

"I said no Andrew. I'd rather shoot you myself than see them crackers lynch you in Jackson. Send that boy," Petunia said looking at a small boy playing in the peach grove nearby. "Come here son," Petunia said calling the young boy and sending him in to fetch the sheriff.

"The sheriff will be here Andrew. In the meantime, I think you're best needed here to get the troops ready. This time around I think Caesar may be in over his head."

Andrew climbed down from his horse and walked directly towards his wife.

"That's the last time you'll ever pull a gun on me. Do you understand me woman?"

"What's up old man?" Jeremiah said as he and Fi pulled up in their carriage.

"Nothing good I'm afraid. I'm just waiting for Joshua, Caesar and Ben before I tell you so I don't have to repeat it. Have a seat. Want a cup of coffee?"

When everyone was assembled Andrew recounted the news of the soldiers and their intent then sat back and waited for their reaction but it was Fiona who came up with a plan almost identical to his with only one small addition.

"For fifty four years I have lived on Three Winds. For half of those years I was a slave. I was raped and beaten and had to live with it. If I had spoken up or sought retribution I would have been killed so I accepted it and went on and did the masters biddin' but those times are long gone. I can no longer look my children in the eye and shuffle along. No longer can we be passive and accept whatever it is that white folks proclaim for the niggra. Those days are gone. No longer will I stand passive while they rape and pillage what I have worked so hard for. We have word that they are assembling and plan to attack Three Winds then I have to agree with my brother. It is time to be the aggressor. It is time to take the fight to them. I say we need to attack them. Let's hit them where they're camped and corral all those that stand by and support them in their attempts to wipe us off the face of the earth. If we're going to die then let us die as the proud men and women that we have become."

There was silence for a long time when Fiona finished.

"I am an old man and my days are few. Sometimes I do not always speak of things that are right but only what concerns me. I fear I have gotten a little selfish in my old age. Perhaps it is my need for vengeance but I do believe Fiona's words have a great deal of merit. White folks have run over us for far too long. It is time for us to put an end to this madness. It is time for us to stand up and be men. I second the emotion," Ben said.

"I want you to know that this could mean the end for all of us," Andrew interjected.

"Then let it be the end. We will at least have died like men and women," Petunia added. "I would say this though. Send the women and children west or north before the fighting begins."

"Who has not shared their opinion?" Andrew asked gazing around the parlor. "Joshua?"

"I have always been with you my brother. Why would today be any different?"

"And you Caesar?"

"I can only say that I am proud and honored to not only be a part of this council but this family. I have some money saved as do a few of my men. I'd like to donate it to the women and children going north and west. And I'd like to see a few troops added to the wagon train leaving Three Winds."

"Good. If we are all in agreement then let's get started. Time is of the essence."

"Fiona could you have Celeste and a few of the ladies get those ready to go packed up and situated. Make sure they have more than enough in the way of provisions. Let them know that their men will follow directly. Jeremiah I need you to fortify the entry ways to Three Winds and shore up where we're the weakest. Hopefully, we can turn them away before they reach here but just in case we can't make sure that we're ready. Caesar how are your troops?"

"We stay ready Uncle Andrew. I can have them mobilized and moving in less than an hour."

"Good then that's exactly what I want you to do. I want you to ride out to their camp and wait 'til dusk. Wait 'til they bed down for the night then I want you to take out the guards, and then grab the horses. Then fall back and wait 'til they've relaxed and sure that the worst is over and then hit 'em again. I want you to do this as many times as you can until you can't hit 'em anymore. Mix it up. Keep 'em guessing, discombobulated, and on their heels. Hit them from the west the first time then the north the second time. Keep mixing it up. Put your snipers in the trees and hit anyone that looks to be an officer or in charge. And cover up. I want you to knock the fighting spirit right out of them. Then we'll know if these are real soldiers or just some rag tag militia unit thrown together. If we cause enough havoc and chaos we shouldn't have any problem getting the women and children clear of here.

Jeremiah how many troops do we have as of last count?"

"A thousand active. Maybe another two thousand on reserve," he said sheepishly.

"Thanks for disobeying my last directive to cut back," Andrew said scornfully.

"That was not me my friend but Caesar who did that. Those men are serving with no pay just in case there would come a time such as this. Those men are not only loyal to Three Winds but to their wives and families. That is why they chose to stay and serve despite your orders to cut their tour of duty."

"Well, when this is over you remind me to thank them for their allegiance."

"I most certainly will do that, my friend."

"Ben I need you to bring your people here. It's easier to defend one place than two and from the scouting reports they have over a thousand troops and are waiting for more. How many troops do you have at your disposal?"

"More than five hundred. Maybe six hundred at best," the old man replied.

"And how many they got over at the Jefferson Place?"

"Not many. Maybe seventy-five to a hundred. It's a small place you know. No more than a hundred acres at best. I usually send my men over there if there are any problems but they've always come through if we had any problems. You know Nathaniel. He's a good man. You can count on him."

"Good. Send word that we need him. And Ben I want you to stay back on this one. Petunia has arranged a room in the house for you and I think you'll find everything to your liking. If not I hired a little girl to look after and wait on you hand and foot."

"Come on now 'Drew. You know I'm most comfortable when I'm on the front lines leading my men," the ol' man said suddenly disappointed at this latest pronouncement.

"I know Ben but you are the patriarch and hold perhaps the highest and most prestigious position among us. That's why you were targeted by Darrow and his men. They know that if they get rid of you they control not just the O'Bannion Place but the Jefferson Place as well. You should be lucky we didn't put it to a vote. Petunia, Joshua, and Jeremiah all seem to think you should be the one to lead the wagon train west and set up the new settlement. I was the one that said no. I need you here to help advise me."

"I'm glad that you all have such faith in me. You don't know how that makes me feel. I am truly honored but the truth of the matter is that although I was born in Africa this here land they call Mississippi is the only real home I've ever known and I will fight to keep my little patch until the day I die. Y'all is young enough to start over in a new land but Ol' Ben is too darn old to pick up and start over again. What I ain't too old for is to fight for what I believe to be mine and I done worked damn near my whole life to get the few acres I got. I ain't about to get up now and just hand it over to no no account cracker at the other end of a shotgun. No siree! Ol' Ben just ain't built that way. I'll be on the front lines leading the charge. And the only reason I won't be there is if I'm dead."

Andrew and the rest laughed.

"I guess that settles that then. I'm not sure where they'll hit us from but I want you to take the north end then Ben. I'll take the south. Fiona and Joshua will take the west. That's the hardest terrain to defend and Petunia I want you to take the east. Caesar has the road approaching and can fill in any gaps I may have overlooked."

Just as Andrew was finishing giving his orders a white woman dressed in all black approached the five.

"Candace dear. What are you doing here?"

"Benjy just told me. Said this could be the worst threat we've ever had. I just wanted to come here and was hoping that y'all could join hands with me so we could pray and ask for His help and guidance in this time of trial and tribulation."

"I hope you don't expect me to pray to that same God that they pray to when they whip and shackle us. I think I'll pass on praying with you white woman."

"Fiona!!" Jeremiah yelled. "Candace is family. She and Joshua and the boys have always been by our side in spite of everything and have saved our ass on more than one occasion."

"And it is those same white folks that are trying to kill my first born somewhere on the outskirts of Jackson. It's those very same white folks with their Jesus Christ that are joining hands and praying that they wipe us from the face of the earth. And why? I sure as shit didn't go to Europe and ask to be no slave. These white folks and all their Christianity. Now when you say 'let's pray' to me I just automatically go and get my gun. No, I'm sorry white woman I don't wants no parts of your prayer or your god."

Candace walked away with tears flowing from her eyes. Joshua sought to go but Jeremiah held him back.

"Candace, I am so sorry," Jeremiah said wrapping his arms around the woman's tiny shoulders. "Fiona has had a hard life and is bitter. She has had to endure more than a woman should have had too. But she's a good woman. She's just had enough. Her anger is justified but her sight is blurred. She has a right to be angry but that anger should not have been directed at you. You and Joshua could have walked away a long time ago but you chose to stay and fight a battle which is not yours and I thank you for it. So, if you would I ask you to come back and lead us in prayer and ask Him to bless us in the battle which we are about to embark on."

Candace turned to Jeremiah. She knew that his words were sincere. Taking the tiny woman in his arms he wrapped his massive arms around her and hugged her before leading her back to the council.

"Let us join hands as Candace leads us in prayer."

With bitterness and hatred Fiona made her way to the front porch where she sat with her shotgun across her lap.

Chapter 15

High on the bluff above the soldier's encampment Caesar peered through the binoculars.

"From the best of my speculations there must be close to seven or eight hundred soldiers camped here," he said to Buck.

"And what did we say were at the other campsite? At least another four or five hundred…?"

"At least."

"They outnumber us by at least five to one. So, how do you want to handle this? Ain't no way we can split up and hit both locations. That's suicide."

"You're right. What I want you to do is go around to the back side and have the snipers start firing away. Once you draw their fire we'll open up with the big guns. When they turn to face the big guns I want you to lay down a skirmish line and open up on them with steady fire. Once we catch them in the crossfire they should scatter like rabbits. But if they get to the point where they can return fire I want you to get out of there and meet at the rendezvous point and lay low 'til we're in position. I'll send a runner to let you know when we're ready."

"At the first campsite?"

"Yes sir."

The soldiers who were now finishing dinner gathered in small groups. Some looked like poor, dirt farmers. Others looked like common town folk who were looking for nothing more than a night out on the town and had found the camaraderie of other idle men for a lynching or two. Several were now enjoying the luxury of turning up a bottle of rot gut and laughing amongst themselves.

"Niggas ain't gonna know what hit 'em," an older gentlemen remarked. "I ain't seen no army like this since Vicksburg. We had close to forty thousand there that day. Grant's army was damn near twice that but we held 'em off for close to two months. Funny thing is I see a lot of those ol' boys here today and there still comin' in."

"We should have killt them niggas off back then whilst we was fightin' them Yankees and we coulda saved us a lot of trouble."

"Exactly!" another old ex-Confederate soldier agreed. "It took all Grant had to win that one. And I still believe that if it had been anyone other than Pemberton leading the charge for us we wouldn't have this damn nigga problem we gots today."

"If ol' Jeff Davis had been there the Confederate flag would be flying over the White House today," he said his cheeks rosy from all he likker he consumed.

But there would be no more drinking or tales of what if as the jug was knocked out of his hand by a carefully placed shot that knocked not only the jug from his mouth but entered his esophagus killing him instantly.

More shots rang out and the cries of dying men would soon fill the air. The camp was now in utter chaos as Caesar directed his men to advance but only so far as to stay out of his snipers range. Following his orders the sniper laid down a deadly assault allowing Caesar's men to advance. By this time, most of the rag tag militia had gotten their wits about them and were beginning to return a steady fire. And it was not long before they too had formed a skirmish line of sorts and were beginning to fire back. That's when Buck's men let loose from behind. This they hadn't expected and were in total disarray. The lethal gunfire tore into many of the remaining troops. What neither

Buck nor Caesar expected was how quickly the sound of gunfire roused the other camp. In minutes they too had joined the fight. With little more to achieve and the sight of his troops falling from their horses as they sought to make a hasty retreat Buck drove the red roan hard. There were five or six militia men dead on his heels but Buck felt confident. Caesar had given him the red roan he was so fond of on his last birthday and the stallion had yet to let him down yet. He'd even thought of showcasing them in some of the local horse races in Jackson but had been warned against it by Caesar.

"Can't do nothing but bring us trouble. White folks lose to that horse and they'll swear ya stole or wanna know where ya got it from. If I was you I'd keep it to myself or just run it against Uncle Andrew's or some of my stock. You're not gonna find much better competition outside of Three Winds anyway."

Now Buck who had been leading by a few lengths looked back and found the riders gaining on him.

"We gotcha nigga boy," the leader, a boy of Buck's age shouted before shooting the roan from under Buck. Buck tumbled from the horse hitting the ground hard enough to break his nose. Rolling over he grabbed it while the three white boys jumped from their horses.

"Don't kill the nigga. I want his babies babies to feel his pain. Let him bleed out," the young man who'd shot and killed the roan said as he shot at point blank range in both thighs.

"You won't shoot at no mo' white men, boy with these," he said grabbing Buck's hand and firing the Colt .45 at point blank range. Buck screamed out in agony.

"They tell me that the worst feeling though is when a niggas gut shot. They say he'll scream like a stuffed pig 'til he bleeds out." The young man said smiling before letting the hammer drop once more.

Rifle drawn Caesar fired hitting the shooter in the back with both barrels. The second bullet blew the top of the head off of the second militia man. Seeing his buddies fall the third man made for his horse but was cut down by one of Buck's men before he had a chance to climb into the saddle.

Caesar jumped down from his horse and ran to his friend's side. Seeing Buck's intestines laying on the ground beside him Caesar knew his friend was done for. Grabbing his head in his hand Buck's eyes opened while his unit stood helplessly by his side.

"Have mercy Caesar. Do it," Buck said staring up at his friend. "Promise me you'll take care of Mandy and the baby. You know she's always loved you. Promise me."

"I promise," was all Caesar could muster as the tears flowed down his face.

Grabbing Caesar's hand and squeezing it Buck repeated the words.

"End it my friend," he managed to say through clenched teeth.

When Caesar could not one of Buck's men, a fellow known only as Man walked up from behind and placed the gun to Buck's temple and squeezed the trigger covering Caesar in blood.

"My God Man."

"Come on Caesar. We need to get outta here. They'll be hot on our heels once they find out what happened and get themselves together."

When Caesar did not move it was Man who gave the command.

"Get him up on his horse and let's ride."

The sound of horses in the distance was now closer.

"Come on. We need to make haste," Man shouted.

"Where are the rest?"

"They're already gone. We just doubled back to make sure you and Buck got out okay. The others should be just about on the other side of Jackson by now. Are we still setting up the ambush on the road on the other side of town?"

"That's the plan."

"And who's going to lead Buck's unit?"

Caesar's eyes welled up with tears at the thought of his dead friend.

"Who's his second in command?"

"I am," Man said riding alongside of Caesar at breakneck speed.

"Then I guess you are," Caesar said his mind a jumbled mess of thoughts.

The raid had gone almost too well. They had caught the militia at just the right time and had killed or wounded more than a third but his strategy had ignored his father's most important rule. Plan for the unexpected. And it had resulted in Buck being killed. He should have planned for a diversion for the other camp; something to keep them occupied. Instead they came like reinforcements when they heard the gunfire. And now Buck was dead and they were hot on their heels. He only hoped that the rest of the unit was already in position and he was leading them into the ambush before they could regroup.

Once on the other side of Jackson and on the tree covered road to Three Winds he eased the pace of the young stallion. They had easily outdistanced the militia and after a mile or so he slowed the young stallion down to a trot before turning off the road at the designated rally point. His men were all in position and Man easily fell into Buck's place barking orders and shoring up his troops.

Once that was done they laid in the darkened tree line and waited at intervals of a quarter mile or so. Once they hit them they would retreat and move a quarter of a mile or so down towards Three Winds and hit them again until they were at Three Winds where they would join the regular troops and take their normal positions. The last line of defense were the snipers who looked down from high up in the trees ready to pick off those who were leading the campaign. It was a formidable plan but after losing Buck Caesar had his druthers. Lying in wait in the cold, damp grass of the early evening Caesar saw his friend's face and the words reverberated in his head. 'Take care of Mandy and the baby'. He'd given his word. Now he only hoped that he'd given the wagon train enough time to be on their way. He would join Mandy later but for now…

Caesar's thoughts were cut short by the sound of gunfire as Man and Benjy opened up with Gatling guns from both sides of the road cutting down those fifty or sixty men who had been in hot pursuit.

"Drag them off the road and into the woods and do it quickly," Caesar shouted.

Minutes later the road was cleared and the men were back in position. The second wave of men, a large contingent, made their way down the road at regular intervals but were widely dispersed.

"What should we do," Benjy asked. "Ain't no way we can get them all in the line of fire. The most we'll be able to hit is twenty or thirty. They're too spread out."

"It's a smart move. And there are far too many to engage with the troops we have. Hit the first group though. It'll give them reason to pause and buy us some time. But soon as you hit 'em head for home. Do you understand? Hit 'em one good round then move out. You got me Benjy?"

"Yes sir," Benjy replied loading the ammunition belt and taking aim.

"The rest of you men grab the horses and get back. Wait 'til you hear the big guns and then go under the cover of the Gatling. I need a volunteer to cross the road and let Man know."

An arm shot up and a young recruit who went by the name of Boston volunteered willingly.

"Alright men. Head back. But before they could retreat back into the woods to get the horses they heard footsteps in the woods in back of them.

"Get down."

No sooner than Caesar ordered his men down he felt a bullet whiz inches from his head. Benjy fell from the Buckboard laying face up dead, a crimson stream flowing from the middle of his forehead.

In all of the raids and bank robberies he had yet to lose a man and here he had lost two of not only his men but his closest friends.

Drawing his revolver Caesar took aim at where he heard the shots ring out from but before he could get his revolver the big man was on him with all the fury of a wounded bear.

"You're one dead nigga," he said lunging at Caesar with the long silver bowie knife. Caesar sidestepped the big man easily and drew his saber. The man though bigger and huskier was hardly agile and lunged again. Caesar parried and as the man missed Caesar didn't driving the sword into the man's ribcage before driving it upwards into the man's lungs and heart. Others in his unit were also engaged in minor skirmishes and he counted six of his own men dead before he reached the horses. Grabbing the remaining horses he followed what remained of his unit and only hoped that the messenger had gotten to Man and his men.

Caesar's heart hung heavy as he rode through the woods with what was left of his unit. In seventeen raids and robberies over the last three years he'd never lost a man or had to kill anyone. Tonight he'd done both. Riding under the guise of darkness he made it a point to find his uncle and his father. Finding them conferring on the south ridge he hesitated approaching. He'd never come back having lost a battle.

"How did it go son?"

Caesar dropped his head.

"What happened Caesar?" Jeremiah repeated.

"I don't know. I can't understand it. It's almost as if they knew what we were going to do before we did it. Benjy and Buck are dead," he said the tears running down his face. "And we lost some more on the road on the way back. I just can't understand it."

"I'm sorry to hear about your loss son. How far are they from here?"

"They were right behind us. They should be at the front gate by now."

"How many are we looking at?"

"Hard to tell. There were two camps with maybe three or four hundred in each camp but they're not federal troops but some Confederate soldiers and a bunch of rag tag farmers and rabble rousers. But it's almost as if they knew we were coming."

"Maybe they did," Andrew said knocking the ashes from his pipe. "But we can't worry about that now. Let's just be ready for them. Are your troops in place?"

"I'll make sure. Did the women and children get away safely?"

"About two hours ago thanks to you. You bought them some time. The more time away from here the safer they'll be. Depending on how this goes we may be joining them," Andrew said his concern beginning to show.

Caesar turned the big bay around and headed back to the place he'd last seen his unit. He wondered if Mandy had been part of the wagon train but it was no time to think about her now. Her man, his friend was dead under his command and he had to be the one to tell her.

Chapter 16

I was still thinking when we were attacked. The steady barrage of artillery from their Napoleons kept us pinned down for much of the evening. They had little to retaliate with but as soon as they tried to advance three or four of our Gatlings would open up and cut 'em down like ribbons but it was a stalemate being that neither of us could advance. When the firing ended at somewhere around eight o'clock neither of us had made an inroad almost as if both of us were in check.

It rained the following day and there was little or no fighting unless one of our snipers saw someone walking around carelessly. Being that we were well dug in and there was little any of us could do I left my post to go and check on mother and make some inquiries. She was holding her position despite being outnumbered in the west.

"They were relentless last night trying to break through our lines but we held them and then Joshua made a pretty good push and we made up some ground we'd lost earlier. All-in-all we're holding our own. How are you doing son?" she said gabbing Caesar by his neck and pulling him down so she could kiss him on the cheek.

I recounted the activities of the previous day and momma did something she so seldom did. She cried at thought of the pain Candace and Joshua were about to endure when they learned of the death of their baby boy. But she insisted on she being the one to tell them. I felt better leaving momma and knowing that she was alright and my brothers and sisters were on the wagon train and out of harm's way.

"I gotta go momma. I need to tell Mandy about Buck and then I need to get back to my men."

"Wonder how she'll feel about the news. Think she'll be feeling sad or relieved?"

I was stunned at momma's rather blunt response and thought it best not to answer.

"I love you momma" was the best I could do. I loved that woman more than life itself. She was the strongest, meanest woman I knew when it came to anything but her family. He knew, like they all knew in the family but aside from her kids and her man the jury was out on whether she liked you or she didn't; whether she liked you enough to let you live or whether she hated you to the point she would eradicate you. But no one loved her more than I for the woman she was.

"You be safe Caesar," she said staring at the ground. She hated white folks. Every time her man child walked away from her side she always wondered if it were for the last time. "And no Mandy didn't leave with the rest. She's at home."

"Thanks momma," was all I could muster but she was hardly finished.

"As Buck's best friend you owe it to him to take responsibility for his family. And if you don't feel any obligation to do that I expect you to take care of your son."

How she knew I have no idea but momma always knew.

In my heart I had mixed feelings. I loved Buck like a brother and am deeply saddened by his death even though I had betrayed our friendship. But Buck's death felt like a weight had been lifted from my shoulders.

In the end, the cloud of guilt I used to carry with me every day was now gone. And he never challenged our friendship. Now in its place came the responsibility of Mandy and the baby. And I knew I would accept the responsibility but the idea of living a lie would never sit well with me. I did not love her.

Telling Mandy of the news was nothing I looked forward to though. We were both at fault. I didn't know how she would take it but the guilt was eating away at me when he was alive and it certainly hadn't dissipated with his passing. It seemed to have only made it worse.

Mandy was at home just like momma said sitting on the front porch of the modest little two story framed cabin.

"Hey Mandy."

"Hey baby. If you're looking for Buck you probably know where he is better than I do. All I know is he's out there somewhere protecting us from those crazy white folks. Please tell me why they hate us so much?"

"Mandy Buck was killed today."

Mandy looked straight at Caesar before her eyes filled with tears that cascaded down her face like so many streams flowing into the Mississippi. Her tears were real and Caesar was glad that she felt her loss and some guilt. He couldn't have imagined knowing the woman that would have celebrated her husband's death in lieu of greater gains. Still, he wouldn't tell of Buck's wishes for she and the boy until this was over. The guilt may have killed the fragile little woman.

Heading back to the lines he passed Joshua barking orders and couldn't bear to see his father's friend when he learned the news of his son's death. This was not a good time. He would have enough to do in dealing with all of his soldiers deaths in the coming days.

There was no more fighting for that day or the next except for the occasional artillery shell firing at us during the wee hours of the morning to keep us frazzled and awake.

On the third day, a bright balmy day, they hit us with everything they had. Parrots and Napoleons roared though the day sounding like thunder and hitting us like lightning bolts. They rushed us behind the artillery fire and there were times I thought we would be overrun but men on both sides fought bravely. We barely withstood the onslaught and momma and Joshua's lines had been all but overrun pushing them back over a half mile before we could get them reinforcements and shore up their lines. We lost a lot of men that day and I called a council meeting when the evening came and we were out of danger.

Everyone was there and I conducted the meeting since I had called it.

"This is day four and we have held up just barely. They are the aggressor and though they may not outnumber us they certainly outgun us. But by us laying back we are only awaiting our eventual doom. What I suggest we do at this time is seize the time.

If there is a pattern it's that they bed down each and every night with only a few guards to watch a camp of a thousand men. We need to hit them when they're most vulnerable. As soon as they bed down we need to hit them and hit them hard. My troops can serve as the distraction while one contingent hits them hard. With any luck my men can go in during the cover of darkness and knock out their artillery."

"That's suicide," poppa shouted.

"That it is but Caesar has a point. They have us rocking on our heels. All we're doing is countering them and so far and from what I've seen is they're dictating everything. All we're doing is expending munitions and with half going to the safety of the wagon train how long do you think we can hold out at this rate?"

"A lot of my men have been asking the same thing," Joshua said stepping forward.

"And with that last assault which really pushed us back I really don't know how long we can last at this rate," Fiona said agreeing with Joshua.

In essence momma and Joshua's regiment had taken the brunt of the battle and were none the better for it. Over a hundred men had died in their regiment alone.

"Then it's agreed then. The way I see it my men will sneak in under the cover of darkness to their main camp and lay down a good cover fire with the Gatlings and disable their artillery while the rest of you advance and hit them when they're least expecting it."

"Let me see a show of hands for all those in favor," Uncle Andrew said his face worn with worry.

When all hands went up I concluded that the meeting was over but my uncle wasn't finished.

"I think Caesar's right. I don't know if what I'm seeing is right or not but it looks to me like they're not interested in beating us in the conventional way but are more apt to hold us here under siege until we run out of ammo and provisions. And with them holding the roads to Jackson they can very well do this. So, right now it's not a war in the conventional sense but a war of attrition. What I propose is that we follow Caesar's plan and see what we can do but the scouts say that they have men coming in hourly. Still, while we have them engaged we need to put another hundred o so families on the next wagon train and continue to do this for as long as we can hold out."

"Give up Three Winds uncle after all you've been through to build it?" I said.

"It hurts but anything you achieve once you can achieve again. We cannot do anything if we are not here. They say the west is barren and unsettled country. The west has not been infected by the bigotry and hatred which we know now. So, if there isn't any opposition let's go with Caesar's plan and put up the good fight under the guise of darkness and get the second train up and moving."

"Sounds good to me," Petunia interjected. "No use any more innocent people dying. Let's get out and give them this old worthless piece of land. But in the fight we take to them tonight let's show them that we are men and women to be reckoned with nephew."

"In case there is a spy or turncoat amongst us and I am fairly certain that there is one within your ranks nephew I wouldn't mention any of our plan until you are within enemy lines."

I think after that meeting we all felt a little better about ourselves even if we were facing death and a loss of everything we spent a lifetime working to achieve. We went out that night with hope, with a purpose.

Later that night momma led the second wagon train of more than a hundred families out through the south woods accompanied by close to a hundred and fifty of our troops. She didn't want to go but was forced to by a majority vote and it was only the second time I saw my momma cry but she accepted her role and momma led them with all the ferocity of a loyal veteran. I know it was hard for a warrior like my momma to walk away from a battle to protect her home and all her hopes and dreams that seemed to be finally coming to fruition but she did taking on her new responsibilities with all the fervor and vitality that she'd taken on all her life.

We set the cover for her with an attack that was both fierce and relentless capturing seven of their Napoleons and two of their Parrots. We then turned them on them shelling them 'til the early morning and using up their store of munitions. By noon it was clear that we had served them a terrible blow.

And it was at this time when they least expected that Ben ordered another offensive thrust that all but killed my men. Already depleted he ordered us in first under steady and persistent sniper fire. The regular troops followed us in and their Gatlings made themselves known killing a good number of our men. The hospital overflowed with the maimed and dying.

Poppa insisted that I visit and offer the wounded soldiers some words of gratitude, hope and encouragement. It was at this time that I learned of a third train of families being ordered to leave under my Aunt Petunia's lead and I immediately went to see Mandy on my way back from the hospital.

"I already lost one man in this crazy war. I'm not about to leave and lose another Caesar. I will be by you side until this is done. If we leave we leave together."

And though the words were like sugar plums to my ears I only wished they'd come from someone's mouth other than hers. Still, in light of the current situation where people I'd known all my life were dying all around me it felt good to know that there was someone who loved and cared enough about me to be there regardless of the account. I knew I had to have her right then and there in my arms to comfort me.

"Caesar you must know that my biggest fear is that what I have waited so long for may slip from my grasp from a stray bullet so know this if nothing else. I've always loved you. Take me love in case we may never pass this way again."

At that moment I knew I loved her at least for that moment. Would it sustain me—us—I did not know but at that very moment she was the strength and backbone I needed to go back to the front. It had not taken me long to grow weary of the sight of pain and suffering and I dreaded the thought of returning. We made love slowly, passionately, deliberately finding comfort in the warmth of each other's arms.

It had been quiet since our attack and we figured that they were licking their wounds and regrouping. On our side we were trying to do the same—rest and regroup before the next upheaval which we knew wouldn't be long. It was hard to tell despite our obvious victory who held the upper hand although we assumed we did.

That myth was quickly dispelled when our scouts came upon fifty or sixty of our men in a mass hanging not far from where we now stood. Word spread quickly through the ranks and morale fell. To Uncle Andrew's credit he recognized the change in attitude and immediately ordered a full attack.

Aunt Petunia and her people were pulling out then and they certainly had time to put space between them and this hell we're currently in. I watched as our men, my brothers, the fathers I have known all my life brought four white captives in and gutted them like hogs and I wondered if I knew these men or if I had fallen off the earth and gone to Hades. What is this hatred that infects us as well? I was dizzy with things I couldn't somehow comprehend. It was all a bit much for me. There are times I can't see although I am looking or hear when I am listening intently. The blood and tears which follow are too many. They cloud my mind and senses deaf and blind, numb. It is all a bit much but what choice do I have? I come from men who fought to be better, brighter singularly as men so what choice do I have but to mask my weaknesses and stand up strong next to my father and uncle. I gain strength from these men and know what it is to be a man. So, I am heading back to the front.

Uncle Andrew has called for some type of twenty four hour cease fire to bury the troops and to tend to the wounded and the Confederate major has agreed but Uncle Andrew has no intention of honoring the cease fire and is only planning his next assault.

His plan is brilliant. He has emptied the storages of wine which he sent to the major and his forces. Once they drink it those that will be too drunk to oppose us on the battlefield will be dead of poisoning. Joshua and two of his boys brought five Buckboards of wine and spirits to the beleaguered militia who readily embellished.

"Say one thing for them niggas," one fat red neck crowed guzzling the wine. "They sho' knows how to have a good time."

Two hours later half of the major's forces lay sick or dead. I wanted to believe it was over but my uncle never saw things as they appeared but saw levels or dimensions. He said if we finished them off where they could not talk it would only suggest the rumor of another massacre and this was deemed to happen again only on a larger scale eventually leading to the death of all of us. And to those that weren't prone to give up the homes they had endeavored under the most arduous of conditions most of a lifetime for the simple fact was that these men's cousin and sons and brothers would return to avenge their loved ones and their belief that niggras wasn't human and then who would be here to defend you? Because he and all the niggas that believed in life full of harmony and peace were leaving this God forsaken country.

It was during this council meeting with everyone who remained that we decided that our marriage to Jackson County and Three Winds Plantation was forever finished.

Uncle Andrew gave the remainder of the residents a day to gather their most personal possessions together and be ready to move out but the remainder of the major's troops and some apathetic followers had other plans. The papers carried sensational stories of a niggra uprising that not only threatened Mississippi but the entire South spread before we could leave and soldiers again stood in our way.

During this time I spent my every free moment in the comfort of Mandy's arms and wondered how I had ever lived without her and then I dreamed of Celeste. I wanted to do the right thing, wanted to honor my best friend's dying wishes, wanted to make sure I stayed in momma's good graces. But in the end I realized I could do all of these things and would always enjoy Mandy's warmth and comfort but the resounding truth would not let go. I was not in love with this woman.

I had time. There was the grieving period for her and I knew that when it was over she would approach me around the idea of marriage if momma didn't beat her to it. But for now I couldn't think about that. I had to focus on getting my horses out of here so I'd have a future when we finally did settle in at our new location. I'd sent half my money with momma to help all them get relocated. And now we were focused on putting up token resistance while we snuck away.

"We have as many soldiers in the field now as we did when we started but we haven't made any inroads into the heart of their defenses. We are not and have never been prepared for a long drawn out engagement. Our army was set up to protect Three

Winds and over the years we've done that quite well. We've endured the threats posed to us and survived the small skirmishes and battles up to this point and defended our lands well. But this is no small skirmish or battle. What the enemy have proposed is that we be engaged in a long drawn out campaign." Andrew said addressing the council that night.

"In other words, and to make a long story short, I think what my nephew is trying to say is that these white folks are here for the long run this time and we cain't win no long and extended campaign with them."

"Thank you Uncle Ben for clearing that up." Uncle Andrew said smiling.

"Had to," Ben laughed. "I ain't got but so much time left and you act like I gots forever."

"Like Ben so eloquently put it. We're not built for any protracted engagement like we're involved in now. We're running low on both ammo and provisions and so we need to put up a token attack to keep them on their heels and start evacuating this place now. The only problem is who is going to be our last line of defense? I know most of you have families that went ahead and are waiting for you to join them so I'm not asking you but if I can see a show of hands of those that are willing to stay and make sure everyone else gets out that would be helpful in seeing how to extricate ourselves from this dilemma."

"So what you are proposing is an exit plan. And that exit plans is calling on us to give up our lives so that others can live? Is that what you're asking us to do Andrew?" Lucious inquired making sure that he and the others understood what Andrew was proposing.

"Yes. I guess that's what I'm asking," Andrew replied his head dropping knowing that this was an awful lot to ask of any man.

"Then I am with you my friend. A man who stands for nothing will fall for anything and I say that he who tucks tail and runs is no man. I for one will be here when the final trumpet blows." Lucious proclaimed.

"I am also with you," Ben said. "I have been a slave and served under your pappy. It was he who made me understand that one life even if it is mine is worth the whole of the community's. No one man is worth the good of the whole. We who knew him and understood his philosophy have no choice in this matter but to stand and fight and especially if you are as old as I am and have been afforded the opportunity to live a full life. It is our duty to pass the torch and allow these young people to live their lives and only pray that they can live a long and fruitful life as we have," Ben said stepping down.

"Thank you for those kinds words Lucious, Uncle Ben and now may I see a show of hands to see how many of you will stay back so that the others can get away."

I didn't want to remain behind. I didn't want to die but what I wanted didn't matter. My dad and my uncle were staying back therefore I knew I didn't have a choice. Looking back I knew that they probably didn't want to either. They were just providing security and a safety net for the many thousands trying to make their exodus from persecution.

So, when hands flew up mine accompanied the overwhelming majority. I was pretty sure that none of these men wanted to stay anymore than I did but felt it their duty none-the-less to provide their children and families a chance. That's all we wanted was a chance to live and prosper just like white folks. And if they refused to let me live in peace then the least I can do is provide my son a chance to grow up and be a man.

I quickly resolved to stay and fight to the death if necessary when Uncle Andrew and my father approached me.

"Caesar we think that you should lead this final group and be there to help get the new settlement up and running. Your mother and aunt will need your help. And you'll need to shore up the council," Uncle Andrew said.

"And what about you two?" I asked the two most important men in my life.

"We'll be along directly," my father said the anguish in his voice easily distinguishable. I knew they were worried and wondering if they would ever see me again.

"They're getting ready now. They should be ready in another hour or so. I arranged for a hundred troops to escort you. Take more if you need them. There's no reason for anymore to die here. When you hear the first shots fire I want you to pull out. Do you understand me? Your poppa and I will try to keep them engaged for most of the day and half of the night so you should have a least a day's head start should they find you out. That's plenty of time. You should be out of the state by that time," Uncle Andrew mused.

"I'm going to miss you boy," poppa said hugging me.

I watched as the tears rolled down his face.

"Now go on. Git!" he said wiping the tears from his face.

"We'll be along directly son," my uncle added.

No sooner than I parted ways there came a thunderstorm of tears and for some reason I knew I would never see them again. Heading for Mandy's I felt better.

"Finally! If it hadn't been for you Caesar I would have been gone. Now I'm so glad I waited. Not only are we leaving but I'm taking my baby alive and in one piece," she smiled as she carried the boxes to the buckboard.

I smiled at her words knowing that she was sincere.

"Are you good? I need to go and see how everyone' else is coming along."

"Yeah I'm good. Guess I'll have to get used to being around a man with authority. Don't take that the wrong way Caesar. I couldn't ask for more. It's just nice to know you'll be around."

Caesar smiled before turning the black stallion around and galloping away.

And then as if the moon and sky were opening up to expose the very heavens themselves he saw her in the distance.

"Morning Celeste."

"Caesar," she said acknowledging him but hardly looking in his direction.

"We're just about ready to pull out. We're just waiting for the signal. Do you need any help?" I said getting down to offer her a hand with the boxes.

"I'm sure there are people in much more need of help than I am. I thank you for offering though," she said curtly.

She was hardly as pretty as Mandy was—well—not in the physical sense but she did things to me that Mandy could only dream of doing. It made me feel good just being in her presence. When we would talk she would make me see things completely anew and outside of my rather limited perspective. That was her allure. And to think she would be under my command for the next three to four months. Perhaps we could have opportunity to be reacquainted.

An hour later, we had spoken little. I knew the importance of taking the books with us and labored diligently. If we were to have a chance to give input in the building of this great nation of ours we didn't need just the passion of Nat Turner and the fiery resiliency of a Harriet Tubman and Sojourner Truth but we also needed the cool, calm, intellect and the great oratorical skills and intelligence of Frederick Douglass and reading was the key. And being fully aware of this I still teased her.

"Are you trying to pack up the whole schoolhouse Ms. Green?"

"The children need an education wherever they wind up," she said not realizing that I was teasing. It didn't matter. She was opening up. As I put the last box on the buckboard. I realized that I hadn't seen any of her belongings.

"Do you still have to stop by your house to pick up your belongings?"

"No that's not necessary. Anything I leave behind I can get again. I am ready. What time are we pulling out?"

I glanced quickly at my pocket watch. It was ten minutes to five in the morning. It would be day break in another hour or so and I knew that my father and uncle were intent on us leaving under the cover of darkness and if they called for an all out frontal assault it would leave the backdoor open for us to sneak out.

"Should be any minute now. Would you do me a favor and check on the older people and make sure they're all packed and ready to go?"

"I'll see what I can do," she said. "And thank you Caesar."

"Not a problem. I'll talk to you later Celeste."

I rode off to meet up with the wagon train at our rendezvous point. I'd ordered every child younger than five to have their lips swabbed with laudanum so they would sleep the first leg of the journey.

Not more than a minute after I arrived to inspect and take the head of the train there came a thunder like I'd never known before and realized that the attack was now underway. And I knew at that moment that we were leaving the only home we had known for the very last time.

Chapter 17

Traveling was slow and difficult those first few days. We had quite a number of older people that weren't used to the rigors of riding for long periods in a buckboard on pot hole filled roads and we were forced to move at a much slower pace than I wanted to but their comfort and welfare was paramount.

We were fortunate in that we met little or no resistance and after circumventing Jackson we stayed on the main roads. Both niggras and white folks came out to see us as we passed by. I guess we were a sight to see.

We spanned more than three miles from beginning to end. It was almost like seeing a city of people on the move. White folks shouted all types of obscenities at us but we were used to it and ignored them for the most part. At other times, some of us would engage in a shouting match. This I forbade but I guess this was difficult for a people who had just been displaced from their homes. But I guess our sheer numbers did more to discourage them from going any further. They'd occasionally pitch a rock or two but for the most part our travels proceeded without difficulty.

Every few days groups of soldiers would come in from Three Winds telling us how poppa and Uncle Andrew were faring. From their accounts they were holding their own right but our men were exhausted and the white folks seemed to have a never ending stream of reinforcements. Our boys that joined the train were all proud but spoke invariably of the inevitable.

I worried about poppa and my uncle but there was little I could do in my current situation though I promised myself that I would lead reinforcements back as soon as I could get them settled.

Every other day I'd climb into Mandy's wagon to get some sleep. But between Mandy's need for attention and the baby's crying it was almost impossible to sleep. The rest of the time was spent settling disputes between my charges. It was an all consuming and thankless job. I began staying out and sleeping with my troops. Mandy wasn't happy about this latest pronouncement but my first concern was the folks under my command.

About three weeks into our journey westward we stopped seeing towns and people and I for one felt a little more at ease that we wouldn't be attacked or somehow goaded into a fight when we started coming across bodies—niggra bodies—who it was easy to see had obviously been attacked. I assumed they somehow fell behind the last train and were picked off and robbed.

All-in-all I counted at least ten or twelve of our families who'd seemingly been ambushed and murdered. I had to wonder if there was anywhere we could go as a people to escape the obvious hatred and bigotry. Sure, I could lead them but could I have an impact on their lives and make it better. It was difficult to see how I could in the midst of such overwhelming odds.

After arranging a burial party and having the reverend say a word or two we moved on. It was easy to tell how the mood had changed and I wondered how many others shared my thoughts. What could I do? I recollected the bible stories I'd heard in church and immediately thought of Moses leading the Jews in their exodus from Egypt. He understood the persecution of his people. He felt their pain and misery as he felt his own and waited for God's direction. And being as I have no clear plan as to how to govern my people or lead them to a spiritual growth so they do not grow bitter I can only proceed in a forward direction and look over the flock as a shepherd does his sheep until He sees fit to send me a sign.

I made my rounds during lunch that day and was pleased to see smiles on the children's faces. They would never know the ills of slavery; never would they taste the unsavory bitterness of another man emasculating another simply because of his skin color. They to me were the real winners. They would have a chance to act and conduct ourselves as the strong African men and women we were in Africa and are fast becoming again.

I don't know how but I found my way to Celeste's wagon. I had no one that I could talk to other than Old Man Micah and the trip was bothering the old man so much and he was always in so much pain that I hardly wanted to trouble him. Wise beyond her years I knew I could confide in her and she could lead and give me that guidance I sorely missed getting from poppa and my uncle.

"Caesar."

"Mind if I have a seat?"

"Not at all. What's on you mind?"

"What's not on my mind? I have so many questions and so few answers? I've always been able to turn to poppa and Uncle Andrew for insight and guidance. Now I find myself lost and with no one to turn to."

"I truly hope you're not coming to me for either of those and I mean no disrespect Caesar but for the life of me I cannot understand why anyone would see fit to kill and maim innocent children like those we found a few miles back."

My thoughts exactly and yet I must hold my head to the heavens and march on like the soldier I am supposed to be when in reality I want to bring up everything inside of me and scream and cry 'til there are no more raindrops in the clouds. That is how it is affecting me."

"But don't you see; you did better than that Caesar. You buried some of our loved ones with not a lot of to do about it. And we've moved on. You made our concern the journey ahead and not the road we have just walked. That road is behind us and you did the right thing by forcing us to forge ahead. You are a good leader Caesar. You are going to have doubts about the road ahead but then you are supposed to. But the people have come to both depend on you and trust in you."

"What they don't know is that I have my reservations and my doubts."

"You wouldn't be human if you didn't. None of us have been to this land we seek. All we know is it can't be worse than what we just left. There is hope in just that. You inspire us all with your firm resolve that takes control and never shows a weakness. It's almost as if you are taking us someone you've travelled to many times before."

Her speech was rejuvenating and I left her campsite feeling the hope I had several days ago after having spent days travelling barren lands that seemed to bear peace. I thanked her for the talk and made my way back to the front of the train just as we were about to pull off. A little over a half a day's ride later I sent scouts out to look up ahead. I sensed something awry and brought the train to a halt before we passed through the narrow passage which led into an open cavern.

There we spent the night. I doubled the guard that night but in the morning all was intact and we passed through with no problem. We had not been joined by any soldiers from Three Winds in the past two weeks and I now surmised them all to be dead. I quickly dismissed these thoughts as poppa and Uncle Andrew were among those included.

We made good time the next few days and by my calculations we'd been traveling for over two months now and had only lost two people and hadn't run into any external problems although there were a multitude of internal problems. The journey was taking its toll on most of the travelers and patience was short. There were numerous fights among us and I acted as mediator more often than I'd like to recall.

Meeting with Celeste for lunch had become an almost daily ritual by now much to the chagrin of Mandy. And one of the worst incidences I can recall was the day Mandy came down to Celeste's camp to inquire as to what was really taking place. At the time Celeste and I were simply having a but Mandy saw oh so much more than that.

"I don't know what hold you have over this man but in case you didn't know this is my man," Mandy screamed at Celeste.

"I'm sorry ma'am but I don't believe we've had the pleasure of meeting," Celeste said in an attempt to diffuse Mandy's anger.

"I am Caesar's fiancée and the mother of his child. You're Celeste and you're the wedge, the barrier between me and my man. I'm here to tell you to keep away from him for the first and last time. If I find you around him again I'll kill you. Do you understand me?"

"I hear you," Celeste said calmly, "but don't you think you'd be better off addressing your man instead of confronting me?"

A small crowd had gathered by now and all eyes were on pretty little Mandy when out of nowhere she drew the little pearl handled twenty two I'd given her and aimed it directly at Celeste. Two of my most trusted men tackled her but not before she managed to squeeze off a couple rounds, one which winged Celeste's wrist.

"I will kill you you bitch," Mandy could be heard yelling as she was being dragged away.

"Quite the little congregation you have," Celeste said trying to hide her pain and keep things in perspective.

"I'm sorry Celeste. I guess everyone's a little overwrought with the travelling and all. I do apologize." But no sooner had I gotten the words out than a scout rode in their horses lathered in sweat.

"Indians Caesar. And there are a lot. Must be more than a thousand braves in war paint."

"Parlay Caesar," I heard Celeste say as if I had a choice. The wagon train was made up of mainly women and children. Most of the men had been left in defense of Three Winds. I had at best two hundred soldiers many of whom were tired and fatigued from the war they'd left behind. No. Parlaying didn't seem an option.

Facing the top of the hill and pulling out my spy glass I looked over the flat prairie only to see what seemed like thousand of Indians strung on for what seemed forever. I didn't know what tribe they were from but hoped they had some connection with the Cherokees since we had a few mixed bloods among us and others who had lived with the Cherokees before they were too displaced. I sent for the one man, Thomas who I knew who was fluent in a number of Indian languages

"Thomas, my friend what I'm asking you to do is very dangerous. But I'd be honored if you rode by my side as I attempt to go and seek passageway though their lands," I said, "Your knowledge of their language would be just another sign of homage and respect and will help us greatly in getting permission to cross their lands."

"Caesar you know I am here to serve in any way I can," my friend Thomas said. And so with Thomas to my right and Man to my left we rode out. The three of us stood proud on our mounts but I must admit I have never known or feared death more than riding towards those Indians that day.

The chief who rode down to meet with me and my envoy turned out to be a pretty good fella overall by the name of Crooked Nose. Crooked Nose understood our plight and relayed the fact that his people had been relocated as well. In his case, they called it The Indian Removal Act and all eastern Indian tribes had been moved to the other side of the Mississippi. And now it seems the United Government was pushing them even further west. Now his enemy thus became my enemy and my enemy became his making us brothers on a united front.

In the coming weeks we ran low on meat and other provisions and it was Crooked Nose that made sure that we had what we needed and weren't cheated by traders and other miscreants.

Despite the obvious differences in our lifestyles and language Crooked Nose and I became fast friends talking at length through Thomas of our various difficulties with white folks in the United States and their insatiable quest for land and property. However and as much as we had in common their stood out one very clear and distinct difference between our two peoples. They were free while white folks had domesticated us and ridden us to the point where we were in far too many cases beaten down. Our spirits had been taken. Our souls emasculated. I never told the chief this. I was ashamed. We spoke of governing and leading men and asked ourselves why we had been chosen for such a laborious test.

We continued to travel through Indian Territory for the next two weeks with some of Crooked Nose's warriors always close by and the chief himself was no stranger stopping in to check on our welfare or often times just to chat.

Their land extended into both Cheyenne and Comanche lands and so they were always at war. And the United States army was always looking for more land and more land meant even more unprovoked confrontations. Through no fault of their own they had evolved into a warrior nation. And yet it was more than a little comforting to know that Crooked Nose favored us to such an extent that there were more than thousand Cherokee defending our passage.

One night on just such an occasion he rode in and we sat and smoked for awhile enjoying each other's company when Crooked Nose turned to me.

"It's a funny thing Caesar but you have become like a brother to me in the weeks that I have come to know you. It's funny because when I look at you it is like looking in the white man's looking glass. When I look at you I see myself. I see a man who cannot fulfill his own needs because he must fulfill the needs of his people first and there is no time for himself. The word I has no place in our vocabulary. It is always for the people. Sometimes I feel like it is all too much."

I smiled and he knew that I understood as some of his braves wrestled with my troops.

"Your men are well skilled in hand-to-hand combat," he acknowledged as one of his braves was being thrown.

"So, what do you do when it all becomes too much," I asked.

"I have never given it much thought. Before I can give pause to think about I find I am too busy dealing with the next problem."

We both laughed because if there was one thing we both knew was that the problems for the Niggra and the Indian would forever be a problem in the land of the free and home of the brave..

"Have you seen otha niggras pass this way in the last couple of months with wagon trains as large as ours?"

"Yes. There were two. Both said they were going to someplace called Freetown. The first one that came through was like yours and we also escorted them through our lands just as we have yours but the second came through led by a short dark-skinned warrior woman as mean as they come. I don't know if she gave the order or not but her men began firing at us like there was no tomorrow. When it was over I don't know how many of my soldiers had been killed or wounded. There couldn't have been more than two hundred soldiers but they all fought hard. There were far too many of us to do anything but win the battle but I was the one that called for a truce. The short black woman showed no fear and came alone to meet with me and my interpreter. When she arrived and before I could say anything she screamed at me.

"We have fought white men all of our lives and we will fight you but we will not be thwarted. We are on our way to the promised land," she said to me.

"What makes you think we were trying to stop you?"

"Everywhere we go they try to stop us. My people think this. One man started to fire and the others followed. I gave no order for them to fire at you."

"You do know that we outnumber you ten to one."

"I am painfully aware of that."

"And yet you would attack us?"

"We have had to fight for our mere existence. Why would my people think this would be any different?"

I explained to her.

"My people suffer the same indignities that yours suffer. We share the same enemy. Yet you come to my land and kill good men for no reason other than you have had always had to fight. You do not know me. I do not know you. Why then would you not get to know me and find that you do not like me or that I have stolen your husband or your horses? Then you would have a reason to fight and take my life. But no woman you do not know me enough to take my life or the lives of my braves. Yet they lie there dead because you did not come to know me."

The woman fell to the ground before me. She had been hit in the shoulder and the thigh but she never uttered a word about the wounds. I then took her to her people on a buckboard and allowed them passage. They were grieving over their losses as well but I understood and granted them passageway through our lands."

"And what became of the woman? She couldn't make the journey," I asked still not sure letting him know the woman he was speaking of was my mother was the right thing to do. We had become friends and I didn't want to damage that in any way. This was his land and he was good enough to see us through.

"The woman is fine. Or better yet what I mean to say is that she is still meaner than a rattle snake in July. But her health still will not allow her to travel. She was insistent that her people not wait for her or winter would be upon them. So, my wife and a number of the other women tend to her. At first I wanted to kill her for all the pain she brought me and my people.

My best friend was killed in that battle. But the Great Spirit has a way of replacing lives to fulfill us. I have come to know the woman. We talk and have become close friends in the time she has been with us. She reminds me a lot of you. Do you know this woman?" he said smiling.

"Sounds a bit like my mother," I said letting my gaze hit the ground.

He laughed long and heartily.

"You come from good stock. I would very much like to meet your father. He must be a very strong and proud warrior to have family members such as yourselves."

"He and his men are the ones who laid down the cover fire so we could escape."

"And you have not heard from him?"

"No. He told me to lead these people away from there and to our new home across the prairie. He said I would know when we got there."

"I know you must think about your father?"

"Everyday."

"Then you must send someone to find out."

"At best I have two hundred fighting men none of which I can spare. If you had been hostile when we met we would not be talking right now. We'd be dead."

"Then I must send some of my young braves to tip the odds. Give me Thomas to make the introductions."

I was so touched I stood and hugged my new friend Crooked Nose.

"My friend's enemy is my enemy. Tomorrow I will send for you and you will come visit your mother. In the meantime, I will see what I can do," Crooked Nose said before standing to shake my hand. He was a man among men and he was my friend. Nowhere was this more evident than the following day.

Crooked Nose said it was because of his Cherokee braves that accompanied us. I saw no reason for the unprovoked attack but it was old news to my friend Cooked Nose.

The soldiers came at us out-of-nowhere with more than two battalions. I had our people place the wagons in a circle so we wouldn't be caught out in the open. It was something we'd practiced many times so it was done both quickly and efficiently. Once inside I stationed my troops at strategic places to hold off the attacking soldiers but I knew that with more than a thousand soldiers our time was limited.

One of Cooked Nose's braves by the name of Lone Wolf who had become quite taken by a young woman in our party elected to light off for Crooked Nose despite the soldiers having us surrounded. I had grown somewhat fond of the young brave who continually asked me for advice in matters of the heart. Now, I feared he was simply attempting to show the woman the better parts of courage and valor. I knew his chances like ours were slim to none but he insisted and being that I had no better alternative I watched as he picked one of my fastest stallions and watched him ride out with reckless abandon.

An hour later the army seemed to content to take pot shots at our people. I'd not too long ago read about the massacre at Sand Creek where hundreds of Indians were killed under a peace treaty agreed upon at least in principle by the United States. Were they trying to make this another Sand Creek massacre?

The majority of our party was made of the old, women and children. Yet, they were merciless in their attack and from the time the battle started there was no mention of negotiations. No their directive was clear. We were to be exterminated.

My men fought valiantly. Under the circumstances neither the odds nor the gods appeared to be in our favor but we bit down hard with a resiliency I'd not seen before and repelled each of their charges. After an hour or so I noticed the officers on their side conferring about something or another and figured they were simply changing since their frontal attacks on us was meeting with untold casualties. But they weren't changing tactics. For some unknown reason they were abandoning their attack. It just didn't make any sense. But they were now all standing gazing at something in the distance. Turning my spyglass in that direction there was a large dust cloud covering the floor of the open plain. It was at that moment that I knew Lone Wolf had broken though and contacted Crooked Nose.

In light of Crooked Nose's superior numbers the army quickly pulled out.

"Friends of yours?" Crooked Nose rode in to ask.

"I have concluded that the niggra has very few friends in this United States," I said glad to see my friend.

"Come my friend. I told you I would send someone for you so you could see your mother," he said smiling. "And don't you worry. I will leave enough braves where they would be afraid to attack your people."

After checking on the old and sick and my people's overall morale and finding them in good spirits I joined Crooked Nose's band of warriors and made our way to his camp. It had been months since I'd seen my mother and I must admit momma looked better than I'd seen her look in a long time. She'd put on a few pounds but she seemed happier than at any time since I'd known her.

"Momma," I said taking her into my arms and squeezing her as if my very life depended on it.

"I guess you're wondering how I fell in amongst these wretched band of never do wells," she said smiling looking at Crooked Nose.

"He told me," I said.

Her face then lost its composure and she grew sadder than I remember seeing her.

"I let my emotions and hatred get in the way of what was right for our people. Now I and I alone must answer for the deaths of forty-eight men, women and children."

"We must not get down on ourselves momma. Leading our people to a better way of life does not come without its trials. No one ever said it would be easy."

"No. None ever said that it would come without hardship," she said staring at her feet. "Tell me is there any word of your father or your uncle," she said the grin starting to grow expecting good news. When I told her there had been no news from Three Winds in weeks her face grew sad once more.

"How long will it be before you can travel?"

Her eyes perked up again.

"There has never been a reason I couldn't travel other than Crooked Nose has no one to talk to and keeps me around just to torment me with his idle chatter," she teased to the chief's chagrin.

"Please take her. Her mouth makes my ears sore," Crooked Nose snarled.

With Free Town only a couple of days away it was decided by the old women of the tribe that acted as shamans and had been caring for momma that the best case scenario was for momma to rest another week and they would bring her along directly.

Momma bitched and moaned hearing this but we all agreed and in the end it was decided that she remain with Crooked Nose for another week. When momma began her protests it was Crooked Nose who stood and changed the recommendation from one to two weeks. We never heard another peep from momma after that and all except momma laughed 'til we had tears in her eyes.

The wagon train under my lead pulled out the next morning and though we kept a close lookout there were no signs of government troops. On the second day after the soldier's attack there could be seen a rather large settlement.

A rolling brook rode through acre after acre of prime farmland and the prairie had suddenly been transformed into plush rolling hills and grasslands. And then a rather large settlement appeared. Growing closer I saw a gate with a large sign hanging from it. It read FREE TOWN and I knew we were home.